Walking in the Sea

To all those who believed in me when the others laughed.

Angela's childhood ended at seven when she lost her sister, but are the memories that she has made for herself actually what really happened?

With time on her hands, she revisits a land of ghosts.

But there is a much more tangible ghost she has to deal with. One that she has been avoiding for too long.

GW00472009

CHERRY VALE GOLF & COUNTRY CLUB

Wednesday 22nd April: 22.30

Chief Inspector Angela Sadler does not want or need to be here, she has been sent. With the great and good of the county, she is attending the annual dinner of an exclusive club. She is representing the New City Division, a pointless carving up of an old established police force that once covered a much larger area. This, as is the way of things, has created many extra non-jobs. At fifty years of age she has been pushed upstairs out of the way. Angela now has a boring pen pushing existence. Angela is not happy.

With her is Detective Sergeant James Parrot (known to all as 'Beaky'). James is a 'loose cannon' and that's why he has never made it past Sergeant. This odd pair are sitting at a large round table of eight people, the other six being two desperately dull representatives from the local Parish Council, the ageing Club Professional and his ugly wife, and Sir Harry Wellscombe MP with his lady friend. Sir Harry owns most of the land around here. He is accompanied by an attractive young lady, going by the name of Anne. Angela strongly suspects that she is an expensive escort from a London agency. Sir Harry has been drinking heavily and can hardly stand up for the various toasts, that crop up every few minutes with unfailing regularity. He has already made slobbering advances to most of the women in the room, including Angela, who is wearing a bright red dress that's a little small for her, revealing a good deal of her long legs and ample cleavage. Beaky has also noticed this, but has been repelled with an icy stare on a couple of occasions.

Around 11.00pm, the centre tables are pushed back and old flesh, which is normally tucked up warm in bed by this time of night, starts to gyrate in an embarrassing, unnatural way. Angela decides it's time to go. The stench of money is making her feel sick. Before she can make her feelings known, Sir Harry gets up, with the help of his young lady, and announces, "Got to take Cinderella back home before midnight!."

"More likely to bed!" says Angela under her breath, trying to put that quite horrible picture to the back of her tidy policeman's mind. Beaky, ever the gentleman, offers to drive them home, quite forgetting he has arrived in the Chief Inspector's car. Sir Harry splutters, "Quite alright old boy, I'm well under the limit," in a loud, slurred voice. He staggers out to the car park and is helped into a large, ancient Rolls-Royce by Anne, who looks scared. After a couple of minutes trying to start the motor, the car roars off down a single track gravel drive, which stretches across the golf course for two miles out to the main road. For a moment Angela thinks of trying to stop him, but decides that Anne would be driving the car and it would be ungracious not to say goodbye to their hosts.

CLEARWATER HOUSE

Thursday 23rd April: 12.15

Angela is bored she stares down through the grimy window. Twelve floors below in the police yard cars make an irregular pattern. A broken mosaic; a jigsaw with pieces missing. She has had enough of 'core values, community targets and designing the future.' She did not join up for this. She is drowning in pointless corporate pretentious claptrap.

She is brought back sharply by the harsh ringing of the large black telephone on her desk. It's Beaky.

"Hi Angie Poos!"

"Sod off!"

"That's no way to treat an admirer!"

"Look, I'm having a very bad day, what the hell do you want?"

"Thought you might be interested, remember our friend last night, that Lord full of bullshit, the one with the vintage Roller?"

"How could I ever forget?"

"On the way home there's a strong possibility he was involved in a hit and run, a man's been killed."

Angela's ears prick up, she wants to know more.

"Are the local police involved?"

"The country plod has been round but he's very slippery, has friends in high places. I've got permission from my Boss to pop down there although it's a bit off my patch. I thought you'd fancy a ride out into the country, you might need some fresh air?"

"What about the young woman, Anne was it?"

"A bit of luck there, the County Golf Gazette was there last night taking pictures, we have a good clear one of her and we are trying to find out who she is. Also, there's a nice one of you and me, I'll get it framed for our retirement bungalow in Weston-super-Mare."

WELLISBOURNE HALL

16.10

Angela and Sergeant Parrot are shown into the tiny and drab ante-room by the surprisingly young butler, who says tersely in a high, almost squeaky effeminate voice that fails to disguise a faint hint of Barnsley,

"I will inform his Lordship of your arrival."

He drifts silently from the room.

"Must be the boyfriend," spits Angela in a loud policeman's voice.

"You don't hang about!"

"I had to wait two hours for you to turn up, so I decided to look up his Lordship, appears he has some form, he's had his sticky fingers in a lot of dark places. He likes the boys as well as the ladies, but he's a slippery old fish and has always got away from us so far, he knows all the right people; thinks he's above the law and probably is!"

Beaky suddenly changes the subject as he stares out of the room through an imaginary window in the dark oak panelling.

"We made a good team once, you and me Angie."

"Then perhaps you should have stayed with me?"

This conversation is interrupted by Sir Harry, who keeps them trapped in the small room. He smells of sweat and strong drink.

"What the hell are you two doing here? I've already spoken to the police; I'll be speaking to my good friend the Chief Constable about you Inspector. This is intimidation!"

Angela stares at him, smiling; she has all the time in the world. She is waiting, taking the higher ground, in control. She is where she wants to be.

Then, at last, she says in a quiet, soft voice, "Last night at around midnight, an elderly gentleman walking his dog in the village of Calvedon, was hit by a car that mounted the pavement on the wrong side of the road. He later died in hospital. We have a witness, who was driving behind the car in question. He has stated that it was a large vintage car, possibly a Rolls-Royce. We are not here to intimidate anybody, but a man is dead. We need to speak to your lady friend and we'd like to have a look at your old motor car."

"The car's not here, the chauffeur has borrowed it, not sure when he will return."

"We would like to speak to Anne, if that is her name; it seems you told the local police that she stayed here overnight?"

"Yes, yes, she stayed the night and has gone off to visit a friend somewhere; I gave her home address to the police this morning. Now you must go, I have important people coming over, more important than you!"

"Much more important people, of course, I understand. They must be much more important than an eighty four year old gentleman, out walking his dog."

"You have no evidence; everybody at the golf club will swear that I was stone cold sober when I left last night and there's not a mark on the car."

"Then you have nothing to worry about then, have you Sir?"

Angela and Beaky make to leave.

At the door she says quietly to his Lordship,

"I have a feeling that we may be back so you'd better make sure you don't get caught in a public place again with your trousers down."

They drive silently back to the city.

Angela stares forward oblivious to Beaky's immaculate driving.

She knows she has gone too far this time.

The Rubicon has been crossed.

She looks down at her ringless hands.

She has no family, except the Police Force.

As they approach the city, Beaky says softly,

"A penny for them?"

"Beaky," she whispers,

"Why do we make such a bloody mess of everything?"

APARTMENT 22

GLENVILLE TOWERS

Friday 24th April 08.04

Angela is awoken by a muffled Pachelbel's Canon, artificially strangled in one of a dozen handbags scattered about the apartment. She rolls herself off the low bed onto the deep pile carpet and crawls toward the muffled sound emanating from her smart phone. In the sterile living room, she hauls herself up with the help of a heavy, vaguely rustic coffee table and staggers into the tiny kitchen.

Angela is not a morning person.

She finds the phone deep in an expensive bag lying on the kitchen table. It has stopped ringing. Angela pulls a large jar of coffee down from a high cupboard as the phone starts its sad multi - layered melody again. She grabs it and answers…

"Yes?"

A deep male voice answers,

 "11.00 hours MY OFFICE!"

"Yes, I'll be there," and after a pause to collect her thoughts, "Sir."

The male voice softens, "Don't bother to wear your uniform Chief Inspector; you will not be needing it. Oh Angie why do you do these things. You could have had my job, I've only got a couple of years to serve, why do you have to be so honest?"

The call ends abruptly as the Chief realises what he's just said and that someone may be (and probably is) listening in to the call.

Angela throws the phone down.

She walks to the window and stares out at the grey morning.

COMMAND SUITE

CLEARWATER HOUSE

11.00

Angela taps softly on the door, opens it and strides in. She is wearing a smart black trouser suit and a lot more make up than she should. The large, multi-windowed room is light and airy with one very large desk in the centre. Sitting around are uncomfortable chairs. A large man, behind the desk, motions to the Chief Inspector to pull one of the chairs up to the desk. To the left, in a corner, sits Detective Sergeant Parrot, looking relaxed in a plaid sports jacket. Angela sits down, tries to smile and waits for the big chief to speak.

"Chief Inspector Sadler, I think you know why you are here, there has been a serious complaint made about you and your sidekick. I appreciate that it was a nasty incident that you two were pursuing but it really was not any of your business. Yes I know you were there last night but you could have made a statement and left it to my boys who know the area and the people better than you."

Chief Constable David Fearnside MBE is a big, thickset man. His ruddy, outdoor appearance would mark him out more as a farmer than a policeman. He is ten years older than Angela and, like her, has risen from the ranks. He knows the job inside out, is well respected and has worked hard to reach this dizzy height; he has courted controversy in the past, but now is looking forward to retirement. He is determined that his applecart will not be upset.

"So Angela," he continues, "What have you to say? What the hell can you say? You've trodden on a wasp's nest; have you any idea who this man is? He owns half the County; he's been the local MP for over twenty years. Okay, he's been accused of a number of things but nothing has ever got to court. I am warning you to keep away from him!"

Angela stands up.

"I'm sorry Sir, I'm so sorry for you because you have to try to sleep at night. I know I've done the right thing in this case and one day I will nail the bastard. So be careful you and your chums don't get pulled down the toilet with him!"

The Chief Constable softens…

"So be it, sorry I have no choice. Detective Sergeant Parrot has already been suspended, awaiting an internal enquiry. I'm sure this little episode will not affect his or your pension; you might like to know that he has stood up for you and is willing to go down with the ship. As to you my dear, what future is there for you here if you just can't stick to the job in hand? Police work is changing, there's no room for your sort of maverick copper any more.

I'm afraid I must put your name down for early retirement and, as from today you are now on gardening leave. It makes me sad to do this, but don't fight them Angela, you can't win, they have too much power, they will destroy you in the end."

Angela makes to go, she feels sick and she needs to get out of the building fast. Then suddenly she turns and says quietly, "I won't shake your hand Sir, it has an old man's blood on it, and I don't need to clear my desk, it's full of crap, there's nothing in it to do with real police work. I have no hard feelings, in fact at this moment I have no feelings whatsoever for you, except that……

I feel sorry for you, yes I've made mistakes, lots of them but I was always my own woman, I've always done what I believed to be right at the time."

The Chief Constable stands up and makes to go towards Angela, then changes his mind.

"The world revolves around money my dear, I'm afraid that everybody has their price in the end, even you!"

"Not me," says Angela, but he doesn't hear.

She is already out of the door.

Angela takes the long way down via the stairs.

Beaky follows ………

THE SUNHOUSE CAFÉ & GRILL

NORTH CROSS 14.10

Detective Sergeant Parrot sits quietly in a corner, staring down at the torn oilcloth covering the table. It has recently been wiped, leaving swirling patterns of dirty water running across the flowery pattern. He is trying not to attract attention but is not dressed for such an establishment. He still sports his plaid jacket and is wearing his trade mark cravat, today a green and white spotted number from a King Street tailor. He has highly polished brown brogues on his small feet, out of place in a world of trainers and saggy track suit bottoms. Beaky is always well dressed and is what was once known as a 'Ladies Man' although the 'Ladies' he now attracts all have a bus pass. He is fastidious about his appearance but not about anything else, which gives him a huge advantage over the rest of the herd, as women want to take him home, put him to bed and look after him. He takes advantage of this at every opportunity.

Once he and Angela were closer and he would have been happy to have settled down and let her wear the Policeman's trousers, as she was always hell bent on promotion. In the force she is often referred to as 'That Fast Track Super Bitch.' Now, he is genuinely sad to see the end of what had been a brilliant career. For all of his faults, Beaky is good at his job. He brings home the bacon and Chief Constable Fearnside knows this. Our Detective Sergeant will only get a warning; his future in the new City Division is secure.

But does a maverick ever want a job for life like the rest of the boys?

As Beaky is effectively on a paid holiday he has decided to pursue the case in hand and has tried to contact Sir Harry's chauffeur, who appears to have gone to ground along with the Rolls-Royce. Beaky has found out that he lives in a small tied cottage on the grounds of Sir Harry's sprawling estate. He has managed to contact his wife by calling the Estate office, where she works. She sounded nervous on the phone and asked for his number to ring back. She has made a date to see our detective at the 'Grill'.

Around 14.15 a tall lady walks in through the grubby door, she is not at all what Beaky expects. She is young and attractive and causes a temporary silence in a room of women truck drivers trying to look like men, and making a rather good job of it. Beaky stands and beckons her over to his table, the conversation is short and one sided.

"My husband, Cyril is somewhere in London, near to the airport, he is in digs. When he phoned he said the Roller is in a big workshop at the back of a large country house called 'Martlets', near Watford, just off the M1. He says the car tyres, wheels and underside were caked in mud and there was some damage at the front. Don't bother looking for it, it should be back in a couple of days and when it returns it will be as clean as a whistle."

She walks away.

Beaky follows.

Outside, in the potholed car park, she turns.

"I've already been here too long and told you too much, we could lose our home, everything!"

She slides into an expensive red Porsche, her tight black skirt riding up to show a glimpse of pretty white lace petticoat. She kicks off her heels, slams the door and weaves out between the work stained trucks and vans to the main road, hiding behind a line of stunted trees.

APARTMENT 22

GLENVILLE TOWERS

Saturday 25th April 03.00

At night,

When the dreams came,

Ghosts walk,

And would remain,

Un-touching,

Un-feeling,

Dead eyes closed,

But always seeing,

And whoever made me,

From the distant stars,

Walked inside the night long,

Until blessed dawn,

And sweet bird song.

Angela has had the same dream for most of her life. Not every night, sometimes there's a break of a month or two before it returns without warning. It can vary in length, but it is always the same, a girl walking into the sea. The girl is Jasmine, Angela's sister, eleven years older than her, who disappeared on a family holiday in 1972. There were reports of a girl that afternoon standing far out in the water at low tide. Jazz was never found. Angela has only hazy memories of this event, but the dreams are very real and she has never managed to cope with them. Soon after Jazz went, her mother started to go out of her mind and died in an institution five years later. Her father fell deeper into his religion, a faith of the bleakest kind. For the last twenty years of his life he had no contact with Angela. She paid for, but did not attend, his funeral and against his beliefs, and possibly his God, had his body cremated and the dust scattered to the four winds.

Tonight there are no dreams because there is no sleep. Angela sits on the living room floor and stares at Jasmine's faded photograph. It's the only tangible thing left of her.

This photograph also has Angela in it. The two girls are standing outside the 'Elms Guesthouse' in a small resort on the south coast, where they spent a holiday each year.

Jasmine is wearing a beautiful necklace in the form of a Celtic cross, an extra print was made and Angela has kept it with her ever since.

As dawn breaks, she makes strong coffee, packs a suitcase and, after a shower and a tidy up, throws on some clothes and makes her way down to the communal garage under the apartments. She fires up her car and drives up the ramp as a large shutter door slowly opens letting in the bright morning sunlight. She makes her way out of the sleeping town.

She is heading south.

To confront the ghosts.

MARTLETS

14.12

Beaky has been busy, he has traced where he thinks the Rolls-Royce should be. He is wearing a sober grey suit, a crisp white shirt and a regimental tie. He has a very convincing moustache and has changed his hair to silver. He is armed with a fake business card, stating that he is a land agent. As back up, he has a friend, who can do a passable imitation of Sir Harry, standing by the 'phone. He discreetly parks his very un-land agent pretty in pink MX5.

At the gates, Beaky presses the button and after a long wait, a tired voice replies, "Yes?"

"Hi, I'm David Porter of Sergeant & Bird, Land Agents and Surveyors, I'm an associate of Sir Harry, he has asked me to drop in to check on progress."

"This is very unwelcome, I have people here. Do you have ID?"

"I have my business card and a letter (fake) from his Lordship."

"What the hell does Wellscombe want? This is most unsatisfactory!"

"He wants me to check on the motor car, I'll say no more."

"OK, OK I'll let you in you can pick up the keys at the front door. This is well out of order, not like him at all, everything's been done, you can check for yourself!"

The big gates open slowly and Beaky slips in trying to contain the grin that is breaking out all over his face. He passes some very large, very expensive cars on the way around the drive to a modern, but rather attractive in a more 'money than sense' sort of way, mock Tudor pile. An elderly gentleman stands at the front door, holding a large bunch of keys.

"Here you are, please be quick then ring the bell to be let out."

Our Detective Sergeant walks past the house to a large garage, resembling a coach house. He juggles the keys, finds a likely one and lets himself in via a side door. Inside in the gloom he spies the Rolls, standing on the far side. He can see even from here that it has been cleaned and polished. He walks to the front of the car and, with a clean handkerchief, opens the driver's door and pulls the ignition key out and puts it in his pocket.

He shuts and locks the side door and walks back to the house. On ringing the bell, a servant answers and Beaky hands back the keys and asks to be let out. On the drive home, Beaky calls a member of his team about his find. He tells them to be quick in case the old guy smells a rat.

WELLISBOURNE HALL

Sunday 26th April 16.30

Chief Constable David Fearnside, in full uniform, playing with his cap, is nervous He is sitting in a large winged chair opposite Lord Harry, in a high ceiling room looking out towards acres of formal lawns. Constantly playing with his cap, he addresses his Lordship.

"Harry please try and be a bit more cooperative with my boys, I've already more or less sacked the Chief Inspector but I have no idea if she will go quietly this time, she never has in the past! As for Sergeant Parrot, who knows what he is up to? He's clever and sly that one, very clever, keeps his cards close to his chest!"

"Don't you worry old boy, if they stick their noses in too far then we will dispose of them."

"You mean kill them?"

"Well they would not be the first to go up in smoke, would they?"

"I don't know Harry, it's all getting a bit out of hand and I didn't want to come here in uniform, what if I'm seen?"

" An old man is dead, he was a nobody, and there's no evidence to implicate me or you in any of this."

"What about the woman with you that night?"

"She's far away and will back me, she's not going anywhere. I can destroy her like I can destroy you David so please relax there's nothing to worry about!"

"This is getting dangerous; we are trying to keep a lid on it, keep it out of the papers."

"Relax David, let's go for a sauna you can leave your uniform here, Kevin my butler will fold it neatly for you, he likes doing that, and then he can join us, you know how much you enjoy his company?" As darkness falls, the Chief Constable leaves the Hall and takes the long carriage drive towards the crumbling lodge on the main road. Just before the Lodge, he parks the black Jaguar to the side on the grass. He then walks around to the boot. He strips off his uniform, shoes, socks and underpants, neatly folding them and putting it all inside the boot with his cap on top. He then picks up a block of wood, a snooker cue and a shotgun. He shivers in the sharp evening air as he walks into the woods. Finding a suitable spot, he puts down the block and rests the butt of the shotgun on it. He rests the other end under his chin and pushes down hard on the triggers with the cue.

At the first attempt it slips off.

At the second it doesn't.

ROUND BAY

Monday 27th April

Round Bay is probably the least visited place in Dorset. Not because it is remote or fenced off, it's simply that there are many more attractive stretches of coastline to explore. It's not ugly, more a touch dull, a wide bay with a stony, slime covered beach. The Elms Guesthouse is now the Round Bay Hotel and is more of a public house than a place to stay. It stands in splendid isolation overlooking a large, featureless car park at the end of a single track lane. The beach is still half a mile further on along a rough footpath that is covered in places by clumps of huge nettles.

Here, Chief Inspector Angela Sadler will stay for the next few days. She has no idea what she will find and feels a little silly, but she needs to be here. Not much seems to have changed. Her memories of childhood have faded onto a much bigger canvas, but now she has time to reflect, to search. Perhaps here the dream will become more vivid? Perhaps Jazz will tell her what happened? After her sister walked into the sea, Angela was no longer a little girl and then, after joining the force, no longer a woman in the sense of a homemaker or a lover and a partner, someone to share life's ups and downs with. She is cold and hard, although in recent times she has mellowed and actually done some nice things for others. As for Beaky, it was his fault; he's totally unreliable, married to the job. He left her when she needed him most, but she knows deep in her heart that this is not true. She wanted so much more than he or any man could give.

Tuesday 28th April

The dream has not returned. Angela has had the best night's sleep in years. She slips off her shoes and stockings and wades out into the sea until it touches the hem of her pretty floral dress. She wants to go further out but something is stopping her. It's the image of a girl standing out against the setting sun almost half a century ago, but Angela was not there and this is an image she has conjured up from hearsay. On the day of the disappearance Angela was taken by her Auntie Violet (her mother's older sister) along with her mother, to Dorchester to buy a birthday present for Jasmine's eighteenth birthday, and on the way back Auntie's car developed a fault. Angela vaguely remembers the repairman saying that a radiator hose on the ancient car had been tampered with. Over the years Angela had often wondered about this, as Auntie Violet was fastidious about her old car and even changed the air in the tyres on a regular basis. Angela has kept in touch with Violet, who now lives in a retirement apartment in nearby Bournemouth.

Angela may look her up.

As the day begins to fade she decides to return to the hotel, the cold sea is getting colder, there are no ghosts here. She is the only attractive female staying at the Round Bay Hotel and she thinks it's time to give the local boys something to look at in the bar apart from the endless games of football on the huge, dusty TV screen.

After a surprisingly good meal Angela decides to retire to her room, but not before getting the country lads excited by discussing the merits of lace underwear with the young barmaid. Angela is tired, but strangely content after her walk. She has no targets to strive for today or mission statements to write up and no pointless meetings to attend. She now has the time to reflect on the past, not to dwell on it, but to put it to rest once and for all. She is hoping for a restful, dreamless night, a new beginning. At this point, her mobile rings…..

Beaky is a little breathless and very excited.

"Hi Angie Poos! Where the hell are you? I've been calling the flat all day. Never mind listen, have you seen the papers, it's in all the papers, have you heard the news?"

"No I'm in Dorset having a short break by the sea."

"Where's that? Oh never mind, have you seen the bit about the Chief?"

"Chief who?"

"Chief Bloody Constable, that's who, you might remember him?

He gave you the sack last Friday?"

"Oh him, who cares, he can shove his head down the toilet!"

"Well he hasn't got one anymore, he's dead, so you can have your job back! Well not right away of course but you see he's topped himself. You and I will be vindicated!"

At this point, Beaky realises he has to breathe and after a couple of deep gulps continues…

"So there's no need any longer to pursue with the hit and run because the old Darling did it in the grounds of the Hall naked, after a steamy session in the men's room! Don't you realise what this means, we can go back to work, I could be promoted and you could be, well you could be….."

He is stopped short by Angela.

"I AM NOT GOING BACK, you can do what you like, yes, why don't you creep back and kiss their bottoms? Yes Miss, no Miss, three bags full Miss! You need a good smacking."

"Lovely!

I'll be with you in a couple of days!"

THE HOSPITALITY SUITE

CLEARWATER HOUSE

Wednesday 29th April 11:00

The room is bursting with the ladies and gentlemen of the press, radio and TV. They are all in a state of high excitement. It's not every day that a naked Chief Constable commits suicide in the grounds of a stately home. There is an air of anticipation, the prospect of a good story that will run and run.

Deputy Chief Constable Jenny Mannings walks onto the low stage and sits at a long table between a couple of top brass in uniforms. She is a big lady the wrong side of fifty. She stands up, looks at the rabble and waits patiently for them to be silent…..

"Ladies and Gentlemen, this press conference has been arranged to give you the brief facts on the demise of our Chief Constable, David Fearnside MBE. I will ask you all to remain silent as I read out a prepared statement, you can then ask questions but our investigation into his death is at a very early stage and until we know more, there is not much we can tell you."

She slips on a pair of expensive spectacles and smiles at the audience. She is very attractive, the 'Darling of the Force' and she knows it! She is everything that Angela is not.

"On the morning of Monday 27th April, an employee of Lord Wellscombe discovered a body in woods belonging to Wellisbourne Hall. The body was later identified as David Fearnside the Chief Constable of our New City Division. Because of the circumstances, the police do not at this time suspect foul play and are not looking for any other party. We do not know why he made a visit to the Hall but I can clearly state that it was not on police business. When we have more information we will supply it to you. I would like to state personally, that David was a superb Police Officer, a good friend and he will be sadly missed."

The people with questions are then asked to read them out in turn and after a few false starts they settle down to work....

"Is it true that he committed suicide?"

"You know I can't answer that at this stage Malcolm!"

"Was there a shotgun found at the scene?"

DCC Jenny Mannings looks at her fellow officers and nods.

"Yes."

"Was David Fearnside in some sort of relationship with Lord Wellscombe?"

"No Comment."

"Was a Chief Inspector of some standing sacked on Friday?"

"No comment."

"We have been tipped off that there is a related ongoing investigation concerning a 'hit & run' can you give us more information on this?"

"An investigation is proceeding; we follow up all crimes committed. There is no evidence to suggest this has any bearing on the case in hand, now if you will excuse us ladies and gentlemen, we have work to do.

As I'm sure you have!"

FOX VALE

Thursday 30th April

Fox Vale is an extremely ugly retirement block, thrown up on the outskirts of Bournemouth in an urban wasteland of overdevelopment and fading Edwardian villas. Inside, it's surprisingly cosy. Auntie Violet's small apartment is augmented by bright flowered French wallpaper and slightly dodgy Impressionist's prints of Paris. There are potted plants sitting on every flat surface with what looks like a small tree by the door to the tiny kitchen. Through the lounge window a yellow bus chugs up the hill, loaded to the gunwales with elderly travellers intent on clogging up the town centre shops.

Auntie's skin has a leathery look and feel to it and her hands shake slightly as she passes Angela a chipped mug of strong tea. Yet at eighty seven she is as bright as a button and full of life, her small blue eyes twinkle under heavy hoods, giving her the appearance of an owl.

"Lovely to see you dear!" she exclaims in a rather plumy voice that she uses for North Bournemouth, "It's been ages since we last met, still I know you've been busy, busy, busy. Now you must dish the dirt dear and tell me why you've got the chop. It's been in all the papers, now sit down and tell me all about it!"

"How do you know it's me?"

"Well of course it's you; you've been digging in the deep doggy doo all of your life, we all have. Runs in the family! Can't keep our mouths shut that's our problem, want to do our best, don't like the Boss, you just can't help it dear, it's in the genes!"

Aunty has a noisy slurp of stewed tea and continues....

"And talking of genes, you really should do something about your appearance that dress went out of style years ago, need to smarten yourself up, and do something with your hair!"

Angela didn't expect this and asks to see a newspaper; she is shocked to read…

DID SACKING CAUSE CHIEF'S DEATH?

Angela puts her face in her hands, Auntie Violet gets up, strokes Angela's hair and says brightly,

"Only one thing to do at times like this dear,

We need to go shopping!"

THE POLICE LABORATORY

MORRIGAN STREET

Beaky walks in carrying a large metal tool box and places it down on the floor. He walks to the office and says, "Hi," to the young clerk.

She looks surprised and asks,

"What are you doing here? I thought you were suspended?"

"I am but I have a problem, like to see Bob I think somebody's sent me a bomb!"

"Where is it then?"

"In my tool box."

"I'll get Bob, he's good with bombs, still got all his fingers, and toes."

She vanishes through yet another door and comes back with a young man in a white coat.

Beaky picks up the heavy box and they walk through to the lab, where Beaky places it on a stout metal bench.

"In there then?" asks Bob.

"Yes, in there, I can feel wires inside it and maybe a battery but I've never been sent a bomb before so it might be something else?" replies Beaky.

Bob puts on goggles and a stout pair of fire proof gloves, he then opens the box at the top and carefully unwraps a heavy navy blanket that Beaky has wrapped around an A4 sized padded envelope. He lifts the 'envelope' out of the box with an ancient pair of blacksmith's tongs and waves it about, looking carefully at it from all angles.

"Only one way to find out," he says, "These things aren't usually very powerful, designed just to blind, maim, and rearrange your face, could be a big improvement in your case!"

Bob makes his way to the far side of the room and puts the 'bomb' very gently into a large steel cabinet resembling a safe. He pours what looks like white spirit over the 'bomb' lights a match, throws that in and slams the door.

"Let's all go out into the car park and hide behind a tree" he suggests.

After ten minutes he returns to the Lab and after another ten minutes, he returns with the evidence, which consists of some charred remains sitting on a tray.

"It was a hoax," Bob explains, "Someone trying to put the frighteners on you, they knew you would not open it, there was some electrical flex, a couple of batteries and what looks like the remains of a condom. I think I'd better have a look at your car, don't go home, give me your keys and we'll check out your flat."

"Thanks Bob, I owe you one," says Beaky, "Anyway It's one hell of a relief to me that it was just a pretend bomb after all; but why would anybody include a condom?"

"Obviously had a black sense of humour.

After all, it was sent to a little dick."

FOX VALE

22.00

Angela is tired; she has been literally dragged around the centre of Bournemouth by Auntie, who even at this late hour is still full of beans and vitality. After visits to innumerable shops and boutiques, Angela has to admit that she has picked up some very nice clobber. A visit to Auntie's friend has also given her a new look with a softer more feminine hairstyle, but she drew the line at having her eyebrows removed. After a robust takeaway curry, Angela decides to stay the night and wants to bring up the subject of Jazz with her Auntie Violet. Before Angela can get around to her sister's death, Auntie wants to discuss more recent topics.....

"I'm so sorry that I have worn you out today dear but we really had to make you presentable, you never know, you might attract a decent bloke at last through this!"

"Through what?"

"Through being on the TV, they are bound to want to interview you!"

"And what can I tell them? I haven't yet received my dismissal in writing and I haven't resigned, so I'm technically still a member of the force. I have no idea how this investigation is proceeding, I certainly have nothing I can tell the media."

"Yes, yes I understand but you will be famous, everybody will want to see your face, what it's like now instead of that old stock footage they will be using!"

"They don't know where I am and I'm not going to tell them, it's against all procedure!"

"Of course, of course you can't, but I can, they can all come here but we only need one TV station to be told, it will be the making of you! You could write a book! It's perfect, we can do it all here and then you can go back and hide at your hotel."

"Tell you what, I'll call an old contact of mine, works for a National, tell him I'll give an exclusive interview, I need to say something about this nasty affair before I burst, but on one condition, I want you to tell me about the day my sister died, I need to lay her to rest."

Auntie Violet's face darkens….

"Oh Darling Angela, oh my Darling Poo Poo, you poor dear.

Why ever do you think that Jazz is dead?"

FOX VALE

Friday 1ˢᵗ May 08.00

The dream has returned, but it's different this time. Jazz is laughing and running across the beach to the sea. This time she does not walk in the water but dances on the waves, beckoning Angela to join her but their father's hand firmly grips Angela's shoulder. When she comes around fully, she sees Auntie Violet sitting on the end of the bed.

"I've bought you a nice cup of tea dear."

"Thanks, Auntie. Why did you say last night that Jazz may be alive?"

"Actually, I asked you why you thought she was dead."

"Because she walked into the sea, lots of people said that there was a girl standing up to her waist far out in the sea that evening."

"Lots of people walk in the sea, I've done it myself, if she had drowned, her body would have come back in with the tide, she was never found because she was never there."

"You think she ran away?"

"I'm convinced she ran away dear, she had every reason to and on her eighteenth birthday she took that chance. Also, I remember her talking about a boyfriend, I think she walked a couple of miles up the lane and he picked her up."

"But why run away, we were happy!"

"I don't think so, you've blotted out the past, your father wanted to dominate her, he wanted to dominate everybody, you and your mother led a tragic life, and didn't you ever want to run? Well you did because you didn't go back home and you never went back did you?"

"All these years I've worried that my Dad forced Jazz to drown herself and that's why he sabotaged your car. Mum came with us, so he was alone with her at Round Bay."

"'Afraid you've got that wrong as well dear! Remember that you were just a little girl. Yes the hose was leaking and the old Ford boiled up but not because it was loose, I had tightened up the clip too tight and the hose split, remember they were made of pure rubber in those days. The repair man actually told me that I should have cracked it up and then loosened it off a bit!"

Angela has just been hit by a large express train that she didn't see coming.

After breakfast, Angela asks if she can hide her car in Auntie's empty lock up garage behind the apartment block.

97A BRANDON STREET

10.23

Detective Sergeant James Parrot, needs to escape. The narrow street out side of his small flat, once part of a large Victorian house, is choked with cars and vans belonging to the media. He's had to draw the faded curtains for the first time ever as cameras are pointed at every window. Sir Harry has been taken in for questioning and has tipped off the press that Beaky and Angela have some sort of vendetta against him. The Rolls-Royce and the chauffeur have vanished again and if our Lordship goes down, he is taking half of the Establishment with him. Beaky (and Angela) are playing 'Piggy in the Middle' but because they are still 'on the books' and a major operation is in full swing, their lips must remain sealed. Beaky calls his mates down at the local Nick.

"Hi Bob, could you do me a favour, I've got the Paparazzi camping on my doorstep!"

"Sorry Beaky, we don't have a water cannon, are any of them parked on double yellow lines or blocking access to the treacle factory?"

"Very funny, listen I need to get away until old Lord Whatshisname is formally charged.

Any chance of sending a police car round to my place and taking me to the station?"

"Won't they follow the train in a helicopter?"

"The police station you idiot! Then I can sneak out later tonight!"

"It'll cost you?"

"Name it."

"We want our silver cup back, the one presented to you at the District finals.

The one that you were supposed to give back remember?"

"Bugger."

HAGLEY POLICE STATION

CORPORATION STREET

14.00

Beaky sits despondently in his cell. The cobwebbed bars on the high window gives him comfort, the open door doesn't. He pecks at a congealed Indian takeaway; although he's frightened of the media he's more scared of his Lordship and buddies. His friends in the force have been keeping him up to speed on proceedings, which seem to be moving at an alarming rate. The news consists of equal measures of good and bad.....

THE GOOD NEWS: Politicians, The Civil Service and others in power that we can group together and call the Ruling Classess, seemed to have taken to the lifeboats, leaving his Lordship to drown in a stinking pit of power, privilege, money, and what many would regard as strange practices regarding public decency. Although the charge against him for a suspected hit and run incident may well be dropped through lack of evidence, people are coming forward to speak out, implicating him in a number of major crimes. He has been asked to resign his seat in Parliament.

THE BAD NEWS: Beaky tipped off the CID as to the whereabouts of the Roller, but it has been moved and possibly destroyed or buried. There is no sign of the chauffeur and Beaky fears that he is dead. Beaky is convinced that there is a price on his and Angela's head. He needs to get away. Beside him on the cold cell floor is a large suitcase, full of what he could stuff into it ready for a new life in Llandudno. His reverie is disturbed by PC Hilda Craneshaw with a large mug of police tea. She sits beside him as he buries his head, not for the first time, deep into her soft warm chest. After a minute or two in the undulating darkness of a deep, airless gorge between the mountains, he emerges refreshed into the daylight.

"I've got to get away Hilda, I'm off tonight going to start a new life in Llandudno!"

"I shouldn't go there darling we all remember you at the Convention, in fact most of Llandudno remembers you, should have stayed on the ginger beer that night!"

"I have no memories at all of Llandudno except waking up naked in Builder Street, wearing a frilly pink garter and holding a very large unripe banana!"

"It was the drag act that did it for you. You went too far when you produced that baby! But by God you were good, never seen anything like it, my husband's fancied you rotten ever since!"

"This is serious, I think someone's out to kill me, I don't care I've had a good run but I fear for Angela."

"Good job that your girlfriend Ms Smarty Pants, the Ice Maiden was not at Llandudno!

You wouldn't have got your leg over the Great Orme that night Boyo!

And where is she hiding now? Or has she buggered off to a new job? Should be here to face the music, got a bit too clever that one, walked all over everybody, sticking her nose up where it's not wanted and now she's got the sack and bloody well deserves it I say!"

Beaky sits with his head between his knees, tries to remember Llandudno and hopes Hilda might let him travel down the warm Conwy Valley one more time.

FOX VALE

15.35

Angela stays in the fragile safety of Auntie's apartment. She makes two 'phone calls…

"Hi, please may I speak to Tom Dixon?"

"Who's calling please?"

"Chief Inspector Sadler."

"One minute please."

Angela wonders if she should be doing this and what she is going to say, she needs to confide in someone and Tom is an old friend. He is also the editor of a respected London newspaper.

"Hi Chief Inspector or is it now Miss Sadler Retired?"

"Well I'm officially on Gardening Leave but as I haven't got one and I've crossed the bridge more than once leaving at least one person dead, I think we can safely say that my glittering career is well and truly over. Look I need to get the press off my back, I'd like to tell you my side of all this and make a statement although I can't tell you much, you understand?"

"Ok Poo Poos, where and when?"

"I don't want to say too much over the phone, I'll call you tomorrow."

"Angela, I'm sorry things didn't work out for us."

"No need to be sorry I shouldn't have been such a bitch, hell bent on glory and look where it got me, a first class one way ticket to Mablethorpe."

The second call is to Beaky, who tells Angela of his bid to escape and his suspicion that......

Sir Harry may be out to seriously damage their health.

"You'd be much better off down here with me. Listen, this is what I want you to do. Get someone at the station to go out to a charity shop and get you some clothes, I want you to look scruffy, don't shave. Get something like an old leather jacket and some faded jeans, I want you to blend in with the crowd and don't keep mucking about with your hair!"

"I don't muck about with my hair."

"Yes you do, you look like an old tart!! Beaky, I know you want to look like a rampant peacock on heat, but I want you to blend in with the others on the Overnight."

"Overnight?"

"Yes, Overnight I want you to take the midnight coach to London Airport."

"Which one?"

"Heathrow, get a ticket from there to Bournemouth. Don't book straight through. When you get on the M3 call me, I'll be at the Interchange to meet you."

"I get travel sick on a bus, I'll throw up!"

"That's good; people will then stay away from you! And for goodness sake don't talk to anyone, I don't think you need to worry about his Lordship, he's a spent force, but we need to keep out of the way for a bit."

"I'll see you tomorrow Poo Poos."

"Please don't call me Poo Poos!"

"OK, Chief Inspector."

BOURNEMOUTH TRAVEL INTERCHANGE

Saturday 2nd May 11.15

Angela leaves Fox Vale, she will head back to the remote Round Bay Hotel, but first she has things to do, meet Beaky off the coach and then old flame Tom Dixon with a statement she hopes might get the press off her back, or at least subdue some of the more lurid headlines from the less sophisticated tabloids. At the Interchange she runs her eye across the papers on sale in the kiosk. Two stand out:

WAS CHIEF INSPECTOR IN SECRET LOVE TRYST WITH HUMBLE SERGEANT?

SEARCH IS ON FOR BONKING BOBBIE WHO GOT BOSS THE ELBOW

Angela is confident she will not be recognised. Despite Auntie's hairdresser's best efforts, the CI is wearing a long dark wig. She is now well over six feet tall as she is wearing five inch heels and, due to make up, her face is a lot softer. She has a white and blue sailor's top over an uplift bra and below a wide belt, there's a very smart pair of navy blue trousers with a slight flare. She looks like a rich middle aged housewife awaiting her elderly mother coming in from Heathrow after a stay at their shabby French farmhouse. When the coach sweeps onto the stand and Beaky steps out, at first he does not recognise her. She steps forward, embraces him, and with a slightly high pitched mid-Atlantic accent says out loud…..

"Oh Guy it's so lovely to see you! How was Florida?"

Beaky is, for once in his life, lost for words and slightly bemused, but finally gets out…

"Fine Poo Poos, it was a great tour, Paula, Scooby and the gang send their love!"

Angela grabs hold of Beaky and drags him across the bus station, between the yellow cabs on the rank and into the railway station. She pins him up against the nearest free wall, where she gives him a train ticket.

"Stay on this side and take the next Weymouth train, get out at Dorchester (South) and take a taxi, here's fifty quid to keep you going 'til tonight. Go to the Round Bay Hotel and stay there, don't talk to anyone, especially the Barmaid!" I've booked you in as my husband, go to the room, stay there and wait for me!"

"Where are you going?"

"To see an old friend in London and try to get the press off our backs, now do as I say!

 And one more thing Sergeant, if you ever call me Poo Poos again, I will kill you, believe me, I really want to, I will kill you!"

Beaky is even more transformed than Angela and is more than a little miffed that she recognised him right away. His shiny hair is dishevelled and he badly needs a shave. The boys and girls at the Nick have done him proud and he looks rather good in an aging hippy sort of way. He is sporting a pair of dirty trainers, stonewashed jeans a size too big and a black shirt. Over this is a collarless velvet dark brown jacket, with gold metal buttons (one missing) that could be quite valuable one day. If he were a piece of furniture he might be regarded as 'of its time.' Once on the train, a woman with three children and two dogs asks if he's Johnny Carmel? He says, "Yeah," and autographs her white shoulder bag with a large felt tip.

Angela has crossed the station to the up side and taken a London bound train. She calls Tom and asks him to meet her at 'Our Place'. He agrees and she sinks back into her seat trying to compose in her head what she should say.

As the train reaches the sprawling tentacles of suburbia, she stares out through the rain, looking at row upon row of dull little houses.

She wonders if Jazz is still alive.

Out there somewhere.

On the other side of the glass.

LONDON (WATERLOO)

15.00

The tea shop is now a dreary Anglo-American fast food joint. It was here for a few weeks in the mid nineties that Tom and Angela would meet. Angela was in court most days at a complicated case of the mismanagement of public funds. You might say that this was the start of her downfall with those higher up the trough. Let's just say that she ruffled a few exotic feathers, something our Chief Inspector has made into an art form.

She has no regrets except that her friendship with Tom had not gone perhaps just a little further. They had met at the court during the drawn out trial and would escape across London to Waterloo Station, where Tom would take a train to his home in Windsor. It never got past the kissing stage and even Angela was not cold blooded enough to take him from his wife and two young children. The fact of the matter is that Angela is a cold and not very passionate person and, due to her Father, does not really like men. The only sex she has ever enjoyed was with Beaky, who was of no importance at all to her on the greasy rise up the corporate ladder. Angela scurries off the train through the barriers and onto the wide concourse. Outside 'Our Place' she spies Tom, still as handsome as ever, tall and lean with a slightly lopsided face. They embrace and Tom says,

"Shall we go somewhere a little less public?"

They decide to find a seat on the South Bank, looking across to the Palace of Westminster. After the usual pleasantries and small talk, Angela tells Tom what he can print without a knock on the door by the Boys with big boots and blue helmets.

"Please hear me out," she says, "I need to tell the world that I am not running away. I am of no use whatsoever in this ongoing news story of bribery and corruption in high places. I am on extended leave and I will resign and take early retirement as soon as I can."

Tom, being from the old school, writes all of this down in shorthand, although he does have a small voice recorder running as a back up. Angela continues ......

"As part of the carve up of public resources known by the snappy title of 'The New City Division' I was promoted to Chief Inspector and given an office job chasing targets and liaising with the general public. As I am fifty years of age and prefer to be a useful Police Officer protecting the public, I was quite happy to stand down, and this I was asked to do by Chief Constable David Fearnside shortly before his untimely death. I had previously witnessed a certain individual leaving a party in an intoxicated state and later that night a man was killed by a hit and run driver. I made enquiries without authority over the heads of the local police and a complaint was made by this certain individual. I accept that I acted in an unorthodox fashion but I wanted to strike while the iron was still hot and see justice done."

"Is that it then?"

"All I can say for now."

"OK, I'll take a picture of you with the seat of Government behind, I can't promise this will stop the muckrakers but it might make you look like the 'Good Guy' in all this. I'd better go now if we are to get this in Monday's edition of the Courier."

They embrace a little longer than perhaps they should.

Angela sits there for an hour, unable to move.

Sitting alone.

In a world of couples.

ROUND BAY HOTEL

20.50

When Angela gets back to the hotel, Beaky is in the bar buying drinks all round with what's left of her £50. When he sees her he cries out,

"Hi Poo Poos had a good day in London sweetie?"

Before Angela can kill him, the barmaid says,

"You're a dark horse and make no mistake, being Johnny's wife and manager, but don't worry the secret's safe with us!"

Angela says that she has had a tiring day and is going up to their room.

Beaky follows like an excited puppy dog promised a very tasty bone.

The room has one single and one double bed, Angela points to the single and says,

"That's yours and what's all this about Johnny?"

"Everybody round here thinks I'm Johnny Carmel!"

"And who the hell is he?"

"I had no idea so I went on line, apparently he comes from Dorchester and made it big in the States around twenty years ago, thought I'd go along with it, he lives in California so he won't find out!"

"Please stay away from me tonight Beaky because I really do want to kill you!"

"But you've booked me into the same room, is this for old times sake?"

"No! It's so I can keep an eye on you! I'll be in the London Courier on Monday morning and it might be reviewed on breakfast TV, so all the staff working here could know exactly who we are, but hell why should it matter? You can still be some forgotten singer if that rocks your boat! In the paper I've left you out of it, so you can go creeping back to Jenny, kiss her backside and get your old job back like a good little boy as if nothing's happened."

"Not sure I want it back Angie, anyway I'd rather kiss your bottom any day! We might start up on our own, The Sad Parrot Detective Agency! Anyway I think that you might be pleased with me because I haven't been twiddling my thumbs, before I came down here I made a visit to the widow."

"That was a bit soon wasn't it even for you?"

"Maybe, but the CC left a file for you in his study, she was going to post it to you, but I persuaded her to let me take it, as I was on my way to see you. It's dynamite and needs to go right to the top. I was going to hand it over to you this morning but you bundled me onto the station."

"Has she told anybody else about this?"

"No, she trusts you, admires you, she knows that you're not bent. She had her suspicions about the old man for some time. She knew he was bisexual, although he would never admit it to her. She's not surprised that he topped himself. He's left her well provided for."

"Tomorrow we need to see if we can make a couple of copies of this and put the original in a very safe place, I'll get you to travel back down to Bournemouth and leave it with Auntie.

You might as well bring my car back, we might need to go somewhere else for a time, but I have something I must do here first, it's personal."

Angela changes slowly into her nightdress in front of Beaky to add to his frustration. He strips off in a gentlemanly restrained fashion and slides into his bed.

He has never understood the concept of pyjamas.

ROUND BAY HOTEL

Sunday 3rd May 07.56

The dream tonight has been different, more vivid. Angela wonders if there is something she can take to stop them, she can't go on indefinitely like this. Tonight, there has been no sign of Jazz, she has gone. Instead, her father is bearing down on her, he is showing his usual anger and is about to strike her with his large open hand. She is reciting the books of the Bible, but she keeps getting them in the wrong order after Deuteronomy. He is about to strike her when she wakes up screaming, "Joshua!" Suddenly she realises that she is not alone, there's a warm body next to her and she wraps her arms around it for comfort.

Beaky has climbed into her bed during the night and is fast asleep. She bites his neck, he turns towards her and mumbles unromantically,

"What time is it?"

Angela pulls him on top of her and wraps her legs behind his back. Locked in this embrace, she whispers in his left ear,

"Would you mind rolling over so I can get comfortable?"

"Of course," replies a very compliant Beaky."

"I want you to lay face down so I can caress your back; I remember that it used to turn you on darling, got you all hot and sticky."

"Anything to please a lady!"

Beaky rolls over and quick as a flash, Angela is out of bed. She then jumps up and slaps his bare bottom.

"Now get up we have work to do, and if you don't hurry up you'll get another one!"

Beaky's bottom waits hopefully for the second slap, but Angela is now in the shower.

At breakfast Angela stares out towards the sea, looking for Jazz.

Beaky plays aimlessly with his sad, congealed sausage.

FAIRFIELD VILLAGE

11.20

Fairfield Village is around four miles distant along the coastal path. There is a keen wind off the sea today and Angela is well wrapped up in her new fisherman's guernsey. She is off to meet Hamlin Mills, who was the village policeman at the time Jazz disappeared. The nearest place to Round Bay is a small settlement named Moorcroft and this is where the police house used to be when we had local Bobbies on the beat. Hamlin remembers Angela and her family and is keen to talk about what happened on that day.

When she arrives, Fairfield Village comes as a shock as it's brand new. It consists of twenty tiny joined up bungalows laid out in a 'U' shape with a large community room, plus accommodation for a warden at the top. Hamlin meets Angela at the gate and escorts her to number five where he lives. Like the village, he is not at all what she expected.

Hamlin is thin and sprightly, a walking skeleton with sad puppy dog brown eyes. At 85 he seems to have plenty of energy left in him. Even after half a lifetime in Dorset, he still retains a thick North Wales accent. In his small lounge/diner they sit at a polished table and gaze out through a large window towards the ocean. After making, and serving tea he asks,

"How did you find me after 43 years?"

"I'm a copper, it's my job, but truthfully, I was kicked upstairs and had time on my hands, all the data on file is all in one place on the internet, a boon that we never had back then."

"I have heard that you are a police lady, quite high up the chain I believe?"

"A Chief Inspector for my sins but not for long, I've been asked to go early, they want to pay me off, I've ruffled a few feathers, I'm good at that."

"As long as you did what you believed was right, that's all that matters in the end."

"The reason I am here is that I need to know what happened to my sister? It was so sudden, even after all this time there is no closure, anything you can remember, anything will help."

"I remember it well, biggest thing that ever happened around here, I still have some newspaper cuttings somewhere, but I'm afraid I don't think I can help you much."

"Although there were reports of a figure standing way out from the land, I can't be certain it was her. There is a theory, well from my Aunt actually, that she ran away, had someone, (perhaps a boyfriend?) waiting for her, but it's so difficult to believe this, surely she would have made contact with my mother at some point?"

"Around half a dozen people gave statements that a girl walked into the sea. Two were unreliable and you may have trouble finding the others, as most would have passed on by now. There was one lad, about your sister's age, he's still around, runs a gift shop in Woolham, can't remember his name, he was a bit strange think he was called Jack or Joe?"

"Well thanks; it was a long shot, but thanks anyway."

"Listen, I've thought a lot about this over the years. I know it's a bit silly but it still nags me, I'd like to share this with you, but I don't want to upset you because I don't think you will ever find her."

"Fire away!"

"Well as you must know, your father was a strange, unhappy man, consumed by some dark form of doctrine, not exactly a 'Happy Clappy' if you get my drift? I had all sorts of problems with him, used to dread the two weeks every summer when he brought his family to Round Bay. He would complain about almost everything from cars blocking the lane to people singing in their gardens, but one thing very strange about him was that he always complained about men, never women. He seemed a bit frightened of women and I have this theory, but it's bizarre the ramblings of an old fool, if I tell you please keep it to yourself otherwise they might lock me away!"

"Please tell me, you have no idea what I have come up with myself in the past!"

"I see that you have walked here, please let me drive you into town, we can have lunch, I need to run over in my mind what I should tell you, it's so off the wall, laughable really."

INTERVIEW ROOM C4

CLEARWATER HOUSE

11.30

"Interview starting at 11.30: Detective Chief Inspector Allan Jarvis and Detective Constable Anita Brent. Others present the Right Honourable Sir Henry, William Reginald, Arthur Wellscombe MBE who carries the title of Lord Wellscombe, and Daniel Pardy, solicitor.

Please may I remind your Lordship that this is only a preliminary interview, no charges will be made and you are free to leave at any time, but I advise you (the DCI looks at the solicitor and nods) to remain here and answer our questions to the best of your knowledge. It would be in your best interest to help us with our enquiries. Before we begin, would you like to make a short statement?"

"Bloody well right I would! (he stands up but his brief pulls him back into his chair) what's the meaning of all this? You drag me here; over forty miles like a common criminal with no evidence whatsoever pointing to me, except from that retarded bitch of an Inspector!"

"Right, let's start with the death of an 84 year old man out walking his dog, not only did this happen on your route home, but it involved a large car like yours, and there's also the fact that you left for home in an intoxicated state and that your girlfriend has vanished off the face of the Earth! Then, the said motor car, which we located, has vanished again, along with the chauffeur, do you really think this man would leave his wife, child, and home for a car he could never dispose of on the open market?"

"The only people who say I was drunk, was that silly cow of a police woman and her demented lackey! Both of whom I reported to your superiors and thankfully have now been sacked, thus saving you from them wasting anymore taxpayer's money!"

"Right, now we come to this other matter, our Chief Constable found dead on your land."

"He topped himself everybody knows that, or are you going to twist the truth about a man who blows his own head off with his own shotgun? There's nothing to stop anybody going up my drive and walking into that coppice."

"Yes, yes, you are right we are pretty sure the death was self inflicted, but what was he doing there that afternoon? The autopsy shows up some rather surprising internal injuries not related to the shooting. We can safely say that he was in agony."

"You are making this up and why do you need an autopsy for a man with no head?"

"Well it's just the way we do things I'm afraid, we need to know why he did it. He could have had some incurable disease. We do know he was in great pain; he would have needed hospital treatment. Perhaps you may care to enlighten us?

At this moment, his Lordship gets up to go, ignoring the pleading from his solicitor.

The Chief Inspector stops him at the door and speaks quietly,

"Two people are dead and another two are missing, (presumed dead.) We may not yet have all the evidence we need and that is good, because every man and woman in this country are presumed innocent until found guilty in a court of law but please remember this, we have a file on you the size of Milton Keynes and the late Chief Constable has left us another dossier of receipts, photographs, letters and statements on you and your pals including one of you spread-eagled against a wall with your pants down!"

His Lordship barges out of the room.

Detective Constable Brent says, "I didn't know about this file and dossier Gov."

The Chief replies with a smile,

"Nor do I."

THE WOODMAN

SOAKE GREEN

13.15

Hamlin and Angela don't get to town but stop for lunch at a country pub. It's quite old but the brewery executives think it should be much older with lots of cheap tat stuck on the wall and a couple of rusty ploughs hanging from the roof. They find a cosy, quiet corner and enjoy a standard pub lunch. After, Hamlin, struggling to find the right words, confesses the suspicions that he has harboured for four decades. It is a confessional with Angela as the priest.

"Firstly, I want to talk about your father, what made him tick so to speak. I believe he was inadequate; meaning he could not compete with other men, or satisfy women. I've dealt with a lot of them over the years, wife beaters, rapists and the like. He would only ever be fulfilled and turned on by being in control, that's why he liked to dominate women. Did he ever try anything unnatural with you?"

"No, but he did hit me a lot. I went off to boarding school after that holiday and I never went back home. As to Jazz, I'm not sure, but she told me that she was terrified of him and would leave as soon as she could, she hated him, everybody did!"

"Right, well this is the conclusion that I have come up with and you won't like it much, but these are the facts and what else have we to go on?

We had two witnesses who swore that his car was missing from around two o clock in the afternoon just at the time Jasmine seems to have gone missing. You might remember that he did not return until after you, mum and auntie had been back for a couple of hours and he could not give a good reason for his absence, claiming that he needed some air. Why not a walk along by the sea under a mile away?

Then, a body has never been found and your sister has never contacted anyone in the family. Don't you find this a little strange?

My only conclusion and you won't like it one bit, is that she was murdered. I don't think he meant to do it, and probably wouldn't have if Mr and Mrs Stone, who ran the guest house, had not gone shopping that afternoon, leaving only your dad and Jasmine there. I think they had a violent row and she said she was leaving. I believe he pushed her over and she never got up again. I think he then put her in his car, drove a long way off and disposed of her body, he had plenty of time!"

Angela had never thought her father capable of this, even in her darkest moments.

Angela has been hit by another train, coming in the opposite direction, but she rallies and forces out the words....

"What about the figure standing in the sea? What about someone, perhaps a boyfriend, who was waiting for her at the bus stop?"

"Well, lots of people go for a paddle and the tide goes out about a mile. If there was a third party involved, why have they never come forward? I'm so sorry but the facts are that she was never seen again and we had a long search plus her picture was in the papers for months. He may have buried her up in the hills, at some remote spot."

Angela wants to get back to the hotel and lock herself in her room.

Hamlin drives her back to his bungalow and she returns along the coastal path.

There are no figures out at sea, perhaps Jazz is buried somewhere but how would you find her after 43 years?

And what would be left?

Except for dust.

Long forgotten.

Deep in the earth.

ROUND BAY HOTEL

17.00

When Angela returns to the hotel, there's a message for her in reception to call Hamlin, who wants to know if she's arrived safely? He also has a bit more information for her. She calls him on her mobile and after a few seconds he replies......

"Hi Angela, I hope you are alright, I'm sorry if I upset you, I know it's the ramblings of an old man but why has she never been found? I've wondered about this for 43 years, I remember your father and I'm sorry, but he was a nasty piece of work buried in his dark and bleak faith; I'm positive in my own mind that he was capable of murder, but, being an old man, I forgot to tell you something else this afternoon about why I don't believe it was your sister standing far out to sea. You obviously don't know that a body was washed up further down the coast. This was a few weeks later and it had been knocked about a bit, in fact some pieces were missing and most of the clothing had gone. The reason it was not your sister was that it was a man in his twenties. It could of course have been the boyfriend but surely, he would have hung around the hotel and not waded off into the sea?

There's another mystery here in that it was never identified, nobody has ever come forward as far as I know. It probably still exists, lying in a cold box somewhere."

With her head spinning, Angela walks to the beach.

Later that evening, Beaky returns with Angela's car.

He is bursting to tell her about his day in Bournemouth.

Angela decides to wait for the right moment to tell him of her father. It's all too raw.

Over dinner, Beaky explains what he's done.

Firstly, there is nothing older than old news, he has bought up all the Sunday papers and they have all relegated the Chief's topping to the back pages, and there's no mention of a Chief Inspector or Detective on suspension. On this topic, he has ordered Monday's copy of the London Courier from the local news agent and convenience store. Angela is forced to admire how thorough this guy is, no wonder they don't want to lose him.

On the way from the station to Fox Vale he dropped into a print shop and made three copies of the dossier. After a very pleasant morning with Auntie, who kept touching his bottom, he left the original copy with her. She told him she would salt it away where it would never be found, but told him the location, in case she was interrogated and croaked in the night! He then retrieved the Audi from the lock up and had it hand washed and cleaned inside, saying that he was surprised at the number of chocolate bar wrappers found in the process.

He then made a long call to DCC Mannings. Angela is surprised to find out he has her private number.

"How many times did you have sex with her?" asks Angela bluntly.

"Three," replies Beaky in an off hand way, "Last time was round the back of the fire station."

Beaky is impatient to get on and tells Angela that Jenny more or less said that he can have his old job back because they all miss him, she also thinks that you want vengeance rather than justice, thinks your ego is a bit on the large side! He then tells Angela that even if they put a case together the establishment will close ranks and anyway, it will never get to court in time as his Lordship has less than a year to live. Apparently, he needs a liver transplant and his ticker's a bit dodgy, due to years of excess. He will have to stand down as a MP, he is up to his eyeballs in debt and best of all, an ex-wife has come out of the woodwork and is going to write a book about him! It's bound to be a best seller and a publisher has already advanced her five grand. Beaky suggests that they ought to send her a copy of the dossier, which brings the first smile to Angela's face today.

To top it all, Anne has been found and has spilt the beans about the RTA. She had been held prisoner with one of his Lordship's cronies on an estate in Ireland and has turned up at Holyhead this morning. Apparently a maid helped her to escape. She was about to board a London train when she was spotted by the British Transport Police. She gave herself up.   Real name is Rita Holdsworthy and she is a very expensive prostitute. The London address, given by his Lordship, was vacated over a year ago. The police believe the Rolls-Royce has been dismantled and the chauffeur is dead. They think that on one of the big estate farms there is a private cremation facility.

By 20.00 Angela is very tired, in fact she is past being tired and starts to wish it had been herself who died 43 years ago while playing not so happy families. The New City Division obviously doesn't want her vision of policing and she does not want to do their bidding anymore.

 But.

It would have been nice to have been missed. Just a little bit.

ROUND BAY HOTEL

Monday 4th May 02.00

Angela lies in bed staring at the cracked ceiling, beside her Beaky is trying to sleep. She wants him next to her but she doesn't want to be touched. She can't believe her father murdered her sister and wonders what a proper detective would make of it all. She grabs Beaky and tells him exactly, word for word what had happened yesterday and what she had been told by Hamlin. Beaky's reply is not at all what she expects, but then she has never had any aspirations to being a sleuth. She pulls him up and puts her pillows behind his back putting him in a 'sitting up position'. She lays on her side very close to him, very close. Beaky, resigned to his fate, gives his opinion of what he thinks happened.....

"I've never heard so much rubbish in all my time on the force, of course your father wasn't a murderer, and how could he have taken a life? In his book he would have gone straight to Hell for eternity, he may have been a nasty bit of work, he may indeed have abused your sister, but he was controlling, yes that's the word, controlling. It was all to do with control because he couldn't act or feel like a man, I think your old copper was right there, he was inadequate in some way and used God as an excuse. So I can't see him killing her, even accidentally, but the reason he could not have done so on that day was, as they say in the movies, because he did not and could not have disposed of the body! There's no way he could have dragged an unhelpful corpse out to his car in broad daylight and how the hell did he get it in the car, what sort of car was it?"

"A Morris Minor, we called her Daisy, well I did!"

"A two door car like your Audi?"

"Yes, that's right, you had to move the front seats to get into the back."

"Well there you are then, how did he manage it?"

"He put her in the boot?"

"Now you are being silly, the Minor was and still is a wonderful little motor, but because it is sort of streamlined, the boot is very small, and you'd have a job getting an eighteen year old dead woman in there! And another thing, where did he keep the spade and shovel to bury her? He needed all the room there was in the car for your bags and suitcases. For a quick job he would have needed a pick axe so did he stop at the nearest garden centre or DIY store? If he did bury her there is every likelihood that she would have been found as a shallow grave would have attracted all manner of wildlife. They are very messy eaters and tend to scatter stuff around. If he dug a deep grave without having a heart attack, he would have had to buy a ladder to get out of the hole!"

And just one more thing!"

Beaky is now on a roll and enjoying himself.

"This body being washed up is what they call in crime novels a 'Red Herring' as he could have entered the water anywhere along the Dorset and East Devon coast. My guess is that he went overboard from a freighter and he was possibly Russian or Polish so nobody would come forward to claim him. The crew would have said he had 'jumped ship' to avoid any awkward questions back home. I believe that your sister had all this planned and somebody did meet her up the lane in a car or she jumped on a bus as soon as the coast was clear. I'm not at all surprised that she has never made contact, remember that you were the little kid sister, her mother was ga ga and her old man was a raving nut case, no wonder she did a bunk! Don't bother looking for her; she would have covered her tracks one hundred times by now and the last thing she wants is to be reminded of you or your family."

"So that's it then?"

"Not quite, I'd like to interview this bloke at the gift shop, there's something not quite right there, why was he so keen to tell the police about a figure far out to sea? I have a funny feeling about him."

"Let's make love."

"Thought you'd never ask."

"You will be careful?"

"I'm always bloody careful!"

WOOLHAM

11.02

Beaky is feeling a little guilty this morning, although he more than satisfied the Chief Inspector last night. He is deep down a gentleman, although everyone thinks he is a guy who just likes the ladies. Most men have hobbies and pastimes like stamp collecting, train spotting and running allotments. Beaky likes the ladies, it's as simple as that!

He's left Angela fast asleep and put one of those 'Do Not Disturb' notices on the door. Last night, he asked to borrow her car and has arrived in the ancient town of Woolham, a place of stone, moss covered pantiles and hanging baskets. Like many old English market towns, it was bypassed by the Industrial Revolution (Dorset had no coal) and today is a weekend retreat for the rich, the retired and the Chinese tour bus.

He parks on shiny, worn cobbles in the town square and is immediately accosted by the sheriff in the form of a young parking officer, complete with epaulettes and a very silly hat.

"You can't park here without a permit sir, not on a Monday!"

"I have a permit!" (Beaky flashes his warrant card) "Now I need to find a gift shop, how many are there?"

"Twenty seven, plus old Mother Barnsdale who is semi mobile and sells postcards from a converted rickshaw."

"I'm looking for a guy called Jack or Joe, he'd be around sixty?"

"Ah, that'll be Joe Grimble, he runs the 'Emporium' on Silver Street, I'll take you there!"

"OK but remember this is police business, highly confidential, code CZ RED, as a brother in the enforcing establishment I'm sure you will understand?"

"It's safe with me Sir!"

By saying this, Beaky knows that everybody in Woolham will know by sunset that Joe Grimble has had a visit from the Plod.

The 'Emporium' is on a busy corner and is the biggest shop in town. It was once Joe's parent's grocery store before the big ugly supermarket was built on the site of the old town gas works. Beaky leaves the young storm trooper at the door and walks into the empty shop.

As the door closes, pushed shut by a strong spring, a tall, elegant man in his sixties with wispy, thinning grey hair, approaches. Beaky flashes his warrant card, and Joe, intrigued, asks him to come through to the stockroom, where there is a small, heavy antique table and two splintered wicker chairs.

"Well this is a pleasant surprise Sergeant! Now tell me how I may help?"

His smile evaporates when Beaky replies in a policeman's voice.

"I'm not from around here; I belong to a department that chases up cold cases. The main reason for my visit is that we need to bring closure to a bereaved family."

"Wow! A bit like that TV programme?"

"Not really, but I want to ask you about the Jasmine Sadler case from 1972 as you were a witness at the time. Do not be alarmed you are not a suspect but some new evidence has come to light (lie!) and I'd like you to go over that afternoon with me in case you may have left something out, please take your time, sometimes the smallest detail will close a case."

Joe puts the kettle on.

"Well, I was eighteen at the time, same age as the girl who went missing. We were then living in Moorcroft, my parents ran the Post Office. It was a nice day and I rode my bicycle down to the bay, hoping that some of my mates were down there. You know what it's like with teenagers. We used to hang around smoking and drinking most Saturday afternoons. When I got there the whole place was deserted. This was not unusual because, let's face it, the place is a dump. Anyway, I sat on the sea wall by the beach and lit a cigarette. Then I noticed about a hundred yards out in the sea, there was a girl. She was tall, about my age and had long hair. As the tide was well out, I rather hoped that she would walk back to the shore and share a bottle of cider that I had taken from mum and dad's shop. She must have stood there for at least ten minutes and then started wading out towards the mouth of the bay. I thought at the time that this was a bit strange. Well, she went further and further until she was a tiny speck out on the sea line. I looked down to light another cigarette and when I looked up again, she was gone."

"Thank you Mr Grimble, you have been most helpful, now is there anything else you can recall, the slightest little thing might help us?"

"Let's have a cup of tea, helps me think, but it was forty odd years ago, a lot of water has flowed under the bridge since then."

Joe goes back into the shop to serve a customer, returns and makes the tea. He brings a plate of Hobnobs to dunk. Beaky continues…..

"You say the place was deserted, can you swear the hotel car park was completely empty?

There was not a Morris Minor parked there?"

"No! Completely empty, I can swear to that on the Bible!"

"Here's my personal number and my home address, if you do remember anything that might help please get back to me. Don't use the internet, you can talk to me in complete confidence, nothing will go on record, no one will ever know."

After a pleasant chat about this and that, mostly that, Beaky leaves. He fires up the Audi and rides out of Tourist City.

It's Beaky who now has a big smile on his face.

ROUND BAY BEACH

14.00

Angela stands at the water's edge, the hot sun shines down yet she is ice cold. She has been standing here for hours.

Beaky arrives.

"Hi, how did it go?"

"Fine."

"Have you ever heard of Stevie Smith?"

"Vaguely."

"That poem about the drowning man, it's been inside my head all morning, can't shake it off. I'm beginning to think I might be him. I'm the man standing out in the sea.

'Not waving but drowning.'

I've been too far out all my life, that's what he said, 'Not waving but drowning'."

"We are getting a bit deep here Poo Poos aren't we? Lets go back to Planet Earth!"

Angela turns and embraces him. She kisses him hard on the mouth.

"Let's make love here and now on the beach, naked in the sand, let the tide wash over us!"

"Please Angela control yourself; I've got my best clothes on!"

They both laugh, something as a couple they have rarely done. After a long silence, Angela is the first to speak…..

"Last night you were brilliant, I didn't realise you were that good!"

"Was I?"

"Oh yes, you put my mind at rest, had the best night's sleep in years, it's true what they all say about you, you are one hell of a detective!"

Angela smiles at a rather crest fallen Beaky, then continues….

"Keep your trousers on Big Boy; you wouldn't want to get sand in your toolbox.

 That could bring on an unwanted rash and you wouldn't like that would you?"

"I think I preferred you as Miss Siberia, anyway let me tell you about this morning, I've got him worried alright and before long I'll get him to spill his guts."

"You mean you think he did it?"

"Don't be daft! But he's certainly not telling the truth, I don't want to get your hopes up, I don't think we will ever find her, but he's got something to do with it, and there's something else."

"What's that?"

"You haven't told me the truth either have you? But never mind, I'll take you somewhere nice for dinner tonight, I'm drowning in this godforsaken place."

"As a detective, in your opinion, how can you tell when a suspect is nervous and is going to spill his guts?"

"With our charming shop keeper this morning it was easy…….

Firstly, he didn't know where to put his hands.

Secondly, I never trust a man who offers me a Hobnob."

THE OCEAN BEACH RESORT HOTEL

19.30

Thirty miles down the coast in another county, lies the Ocean Beach Resort Hotel which doesn't exactly lie; instead it sort of props itself up on a low headland. This huge Victorian monolith was built by an over optimistic railway company, who hoped the masses would come here to enjoy the seaside and this would create a new resort on acres of the barren wilderness they had bought nearby. Unfortunately, the place was called Fullers Drove and even after renaming, by the GWR to Riviera Sands, it never really prospered. This was not helped by the nearest railway station being over ten miles away. During the Great War it became an isolation hospital and remained as such until the sixties. It was then turned into an outward bound centre for city kids. Later, it was abandoned to the elements and threatened with demolition until some idiot persuaded the powers that be that it was of architectural merit, and a preservation order was slapped on the ugly old money pit. Recently, it has been bought, along with a few more life-expired, crumbling ruins around the country, by the American hotel & restaurant chain, Swagger Resort Hotels Inc, and has had a complete make over. This refurbishment is not to everybody's taste but the food is expensive and nice.

Beaky plays with his prawn cocktail, while an impressed Angela wolfs down the excellent garlic mushroom supreme. Beaky is not known for spending money, but he clearly has something on his mind to push the boat out this far. After the wonderfully inventive Fisherman's Platter Americana followed by a Riviera Fruit Salad de Ville to die for, Beaky suggests that they repair to the lounge for coffee. He suggests that Angela calls Round Bay and tells them they will be back tomorrow. He's already booked a room here for the night. Angela is impressed, but worried, he's normally such a cheerful soul. After sitting in silence for half an hour, she asks,

"What's up?"

Beaky replies,

"Will you marry me?"

"Well maybe but I'm not going to Bognor Regis!"

"Alright then, how about Bournemouth? I'm going to have to go back home for a few days, I've had a couple of 'phone calls this afternoon. I'm worried about you, forget about the marriage, it wouldn't work anyway, but I don't want you staying at Round Bay on your own, can you stay with Auntie until I get back? It would put my mind at rest."

"I've just about had enough of this beating around the bush! Spit it out! Spit it out!"

"I've had a couple of 'phone calls."

"Yes and we all know who from! That broody old hen Jenny Mannings is on heat, she wants you back, they've had high level talks at HQ, can't do without you, wants you to have her up against the wall again at the ambulance station!"

"It was a fire station!"

"Well go then, you are obviously not on suspension anymore, and you can tell the old cow that I'm not coming back to sit in an office all day!"

"Actually, it's not quite like that and Jenny is not an old cow, you might remember that you and her were best mates at one time so that was uncalled for, jealousy is a nasty thing."

"I am not jealous, but you are right, I'm the stupid cow. She will make an excellent and honest Chief, I'm sorry but you really are starting to wind me up tonight."

"The reason they have asked me to return is that they want to offer me a new job setting up a new team. So yes, basically I can have my old job back but I won't take it. This last week of freedom has convinced me to retire early. I'll have a nice pension and so will you. I can take on a little light detective work in my spare time and you will have no trouble at all getting a consultancy job after that write up about you in the London Courier. Now this case against his Lordship is slotting nicely into place you are coming out of all this smelling like roses and rightly so. You are the best Poo Poos, you always were. They certainly got their money's worth out of you!"

"So you now want me to marry you so you can be my sissy maid in Bognor Regis?"

"It's Bournemouth."

"Don't change the subject!"

"I could do a little light dusting and you could supply me with a pretty uniform. If I missed a bit now and then, you could slap my bottom!"

"That was twenty five years ago, we've all grown up since then!"

"No, you have!"

"Alright, what was the other 'phone call then?"

"Ah, that one concerns you; it was from our Joe, he has something to tell me, but I'll let him stew until I get back. As they say, 'A little wait makes the soul feel guiltier'. He wanted to put it all on a CD and send it to me, but I said no because....

They normally top themselves after doing that!"

THE THOMAS HARDY SUITE

THIRD FLOOR

THE OCEAN BEACH RESORT HOTEL

Midnight

Beaky has thoughtfully brought along a washing kit and a silk nightdress that he's taken from Angela's drawer back at the Round Bay Hotel. They lay wide apart in the king size bed.

Angela is the first to break the silence…….

"I wish you wouldn't wear that nightdress it doesn't suit you, I know all about Llandudno."

"I wish I could remember Llandudno."

"What did you mean this afternoon when you said that I was not telling the truth?"

"Well you're not are you? You don't have to be a detective to work that one out. Your sister vanished 43 years ago, you hardly remember her and you think she's dead because a boy saw someone standing in the sea. The girl that you're looking for walking in the sea is not her, the girl you are looking for is you, a fantasised version of you, a you with a loving mum and dad playing happy families in a world that doesn't exist. A world you have made up to block out something that may have happened in your bloody awful childhood."

Angela moves in closer and grabs Beaky by his hair.

"You think you are such a bloody good detective don't you? So you think the girl I'm looking for is me do you? Well you are so wrong! I should have told you this twenty five years ago but you weren't there, remember that? You weren't there when I needed you! OK it takes two to tango, it's my fault, I wanted to go to the top and I almost got there! The girl I'm looking for I know I'll never find. BECAUSE THE LITTLE GIRL I'M LOOKING FOR IS OUR DAUGHTER. Yes our daughter, our daughter, our daughter, our daughter……

Angela pushes her face deep into her pillow. The cries become howls as the pain is released.

Beaky goes to touch her.

"Don't touch me! I'm evil I gave her away! I held her in my arms, I carried her for nine months, and then I gave her away! My life on the Force was more important than my own flesh and blood, what sort of mother does that make me? What could I do? My own mother was dead, my father had disowned me, and you were not there!

At the time, I wanted the best for her. If you want to marry me as you say you do, if you want to help me, and if you really love me, if you want to play happy families then I WANT YOU TO TRY AND FIND HER! I'll give you the scant details, it's all I have but don't come back until you've found her understand?

No, no that's unfair I'm sorry, just do your best but promise me one thing. If you find her please don't tell her about me, I never want to see her, I can't see her you understand? I can never face her but I just want to know she's OK. I never, ever want to meet her, you understand this? You must understand, I just want to know where she is, perhaps you could get a photograph that I can keep with my other one."

BOURNEMOUTH

Tuesday 5th May

When Angela awakes, Beaky has gone. He's paid the bill and left a note by the car keys.

Dear Poo Poos

I will be away for a few days, please, please email or text with all you know about our daughter. As you can imagine, this has come as a bit of a shock to say the least. I will do my best to trace her and start by ringing round all my contacts; at least we will have a better chance of finding her than we have with your sister. I promise I will not tell her where you are. I hope you feel better this morning, I should imagine a huge weight has been lifted from you and you can now look forward to the future and move on.

I'll call tonight, promise me you will leave Round Bay, there is nothing there for you.

Please take care

James

By late morning Angela is well on the way to Auntie Violet's. She has stowed the top and is driving fast, enjoying the breeze running through her hair. Although, in the pit of her stomach, she is starting to regret telling Beaky about the baby, in her heart of hearts she knows that she had to tell him one day. She hates to admit it but a huge burden has been lifted from her. At Auntie's apartment she sends off, from her laptop, the details of her daughter's birth, twenty five years ago. She then tells

Auntie, who is thrilled to have been a Great Aunt all these years without knowing it!

Beaky has taken a taxi to the station and arrives home in the late afternoon. In the evening, he calls Angela.

JENNY MANNINGS' OFFICE

CLEARWATER HOUSE

Wednesday 6th May 14.30

Beaky has spent the morning cleaning and tidying his small flat.

Beaky likes everything to be in its place and he has a place for everything. He has decided to put his home, for the last thirty years, on the market. It's a wrench, he was born just two streets away and has lived in this small town all of his life. But now, because he has decided to leave the force, he wants to make a clean sweep. He would like to spend his remaining years by the sea. For his interview with DCC Mannings, he has put on his best funereal suit, a crisp white shirt and a federation tie. His shoes are polished and even his socks match. Arriving outside the Chief's office at precisely 14.25 he checks himself over in a small mirror that he carries with him at all times. At 14.30, a beaming Jenny opens the door and invites him in.

DCC Mannings is dressed in full uniform, which Beaky has always found a bit of a turn on. This does not show on his face as they partake in a little social intercourse around the Mulberry bush before getting down to business. Jenny starts the ball rolling……

"I'm sure you know why I want to see you, we have considered what's happened recently and have come to the conclusion that none of this nasty business is your fault! OK, you did help Angie to go for the jugular, which you knew she would and it was just a bit unfortunate that she asked you to go to that god awful party and that was the Chief's fault for trying to win brownie points with the County Set, not a lot of good it did him! So welcome back into the fold with a promotion to Inspector for the time being, a rise in salary and a new office! They pulled somebody out of the canal last night so you can start on that one right away! Now what do you think about that? We can go out tonight and celebrate."

Beaky considers for a few seconds.....

"Sorry Marm, but no. This last week with Poo Poos I've had time to think and I've realised that I've had enough. I've had enough of the bloody 'Establishment' and the 'Old Boy Network'. I should never have been suspended, I was just doing my job, after all an old man had been killed and nobody cared except the Chief Inspector. Yes I agree perhaps she is a bit too honest and has this self destruct tendency, but she cared about justice, nobody else did!"

"I'm surprised to hear you talk like that James, as there's never been any love lost between you two has there? You make the 'Odd Couple' look like 'Romeo and Juliet'."

"Maybe, maybe not, but she needs me, I'm all she's got for the time being, I have my letter of resignation here. As far as I'm concerned I'm still on suspension and I don't particularly want to work out my notice!" I will, however, have a look into this body that's been fished out of the cut if you want?

Jenny goes very quiet, stands and walks around behind him. She kisses his neck and softly says.....

"If that's the way you want it Sweety Pie, but let's go out tonight, somewhere out of the way.

Just for old time's sake Plonkey."

BOSCOMBE PIER

15.15

Boscombe Pier has always been a poor relation to Bournemouth Pier and has never really got over World War Two, when it was blown up by the wrong side, as it could have saved an invading army getting their feet wet. Angela came here once or twice when her parents were visiting Auntie Violet. In those days, Auntie lived in a rambling old Edwardian house that reeked of cats in a dusty Boscombe back street. The pier had a bit of a revival at that time and for a few years a roller skating rink was established in the pavilion at the seaward end. Angela was not allowed to skate, as the family God took a dim view about doing anything like that for pleasure, but today she remembers the music and the noise made by the young crowd on their old fashioned wooden skates. Today, the pier is open to the sky and makes a wonderful free trip onto the ocean for some sea air. At the far end, before she returns to land Ray Charles is singing 'I Can't Stop Loving You' and the wooden skates are rumbling and sliding on the old dance floor inside her head.

Auntie does not trust her safety to the pier and remains on the Undercliff. She sits on a bench knitting baby clothes for her newly discovered granddaughter, who would now be twenty five years of age. At first, she kept pressing her niece about the baby, but after seeing the pain it was causing, has decided to knit instead. Although never married and childless, Auntie has had her moments and indeed has a boyfriend, who is away on a bowls tour. She is a bit worried about explaining nights away, if Angela stays much longer.

On their way back to the car, Auntie suggests going to the shops.

"I want to buy a nice picture frame dear, for when Beaky gets back with your little girl's photograph, I know and I really do understand dear, why you can't meet her face to face, but it would please an old woman who's never had a child of her own to have just one picture."

"You are placing a lot of faith in James, Auntie. He may be a good detective but he's not Superman, I don't even know if he will even try!"

"Oh yes he will," says Auntie with a smile.

You see, he is Superman.

He's your Superman.

He always will be."

KASEY'S WINEBAR

CHURCH HILL

20.45

Jenny and Beaky sit away from the bar. Candlelight throws moving patterns along the low barrel ceiling. Beaky has not been here before, but Jenny seems to be well known.

"I wanted to get well away from HQ; they don't know round here that I'm a policeman!"

"I'm glad because I want to discuss something very confidential; I want to tell you a secret."

"My you're getting my juices running tonight James; I've never thought of you being secretive but if you need to unburden yourself please feel free to shoot."

"You're not wired up are you?"

"You mean my bra, would you like to check it out?"

"No I mean that you're not carrying anything that can record our conversation or send it to God knows where?"

"Good Lord, what kind of world do you live in? Of course I'm not, I'm taking a chance, I've got a hell of a lot more to lose than you, including a husband of thirty seven years!

I'm taking a big chance being here with you!"

Beaky looks around and leans across the table. After moving a large candle and holder, he whispers.......

"Did you know that Angela had a baby back in 1990?"

Jenny goes very quiet as she tries to put an answer together.

"What I am going to tell you James is strictly confidential because it was all hushed up at the time; she was too good to lose, so she was given the best part of a year off. We knew she could not keep the baby, let's face it, she's hardly Miss Motherhood 1990 is she? So why does she now want to play the Waltons?"

" I think her conscience may be nagging her, she does not want to meet the girl, just wants to know if she's alright. I'm supposed to get in contact. I don't suppose you know where she is?"

"Of course I do, we got the baby adopted by a PC and his wife, lovely couple as I recall, who couldn't have kids, such a shame"

"How the hell did you do all this?"

"I was PA then to old Battleaxe Bertha, you must remember her? Anyway, she had a heart of gold and we all kept our mouths shut. In those days she was in charge of what they now call Human Resources. Do you want to know who Daddy is?"

"Angela says it's me and the dates all work out right but I can't be sure, she was in a bit of a state when she told me!"

"You have that effect on us girls James but I don't think there's much doubt as she is your spitting image right down to the shiny shoes, and at times she can be a right pain up the backside!"

"So you know where she is?"

"Of course, I'm her favourite Auntie!"

"That's great, tell me where she is and I can get back to Angie by the weekend!"

"Not so fast, I deserve something in return."

"Like what?"

"Well firstly I've booked us a room at the motel down the road, the Old Man thinks I'm in Leeds on a conference, so you will have to be nice to me Plonkey, Plonkey!"

"Can't do it, I haven't bought my toothbrush!"

"You should remember that on the motorway you can get all that sort of stuff out of a vending machine in the gentlemen's washroom. Don't worry, I'll tell you what you want to know but why be in a hurry? I've bought the lasso and the boots. I've even got the sheriff's badge and the handcuffs."

"Can I wear the white hat?"

"Hi ho Silvo!"

97A BRANDON STREET

Thursday 7th May 12.00

Beaky gets back to the flat around midday, it's been a long drive through heavy rain, bringing the motorway to a halt at times. On the way into town, he's made a visit to the local estate agent and they are coming round to look at the place later today. He is intrigued to find a letter with a Dorset postmark among the usual rubbish. He is not surprised to find that it's from Joe Grimble but is surprised to find a key wrapped up in greaseproof paper with a letter written on an ancient typewriter.

6th May

Dear Detective Sergeant Parrot

Please find enclosed a key to the back door of my shop in Woolham.

I will be away for around six weeks, but I promise to return. I have decided to sell up my assets here and live out my remaining years in the sun. I am not trying to get away without being punished but I was eighteen with all the arrogance of youth. As to what took place, it is now forty three years ago, what would punishing me achieve? I know that you are a good and fair minded man and will do what you think is best. I have made and signed a statement which, I hope, will bring closure to the family involved.

As you enter the storeroom of my shop, to your right you will see the heavy old coffee table by which we sat the other day. Under this table are a couple of loose floorboards. Pull them up (you may need a big screwdriver) and then reach down to retrieve a black, steel cash box. Open the box and inside I have left a large brown envelope, which contains my statement.

I'm not proud of what I did and I've thought about it every day since.

I wish that I could change the past.

I was just in the wrong place at the wrong time.

Yours sincerely

Joseph Clark Grimble

Beaky has already worked out in his mind what might have happened? Beaky wants to get back to Angela and sort this mess out.

It is now raining even harder.

CITY MORTUARY

17.50

Beaky has dealt with the Estate Agent and has had a call from Jenny, asking him to pop in and look at the victim found in the canal. When he asked about Angela's child he was told that she was not answering her 'phone but Jenny explains, "We'll have another go tomorrow, I've left a message to ring 'Auntie Jen' urgently!"

Beaky does not need to find the morgue; he's been there before. He's never been too happy being near dead bodies, especially when they have been immersed in stagnant water. It's not quite so bad today, as according to the preliminary report, the remains have only been in the water for a couple of hours or so before they were discovered. It's a young man in his early twenties, athletic and muscular. He carries pointless tattoos across most of his body and wears a heavy gold earring on his left earlobe. His clothes, when found, were expensive designer stuff and he was wearing top quality trainers. There is no sign on the body of a struggle and it looks like he fell in the canal and drank too much water, although Beaky strongly suspects that he was pushed in by more than one person.

Detective Sergeant Welland, one of Beaky's contemporaries, asks,

"Recognise him Beaky?"

"Yes, it's Jason Bishop, better known as 'The Preacher' because of his big mouth. He was a nasty bit of work and I'm not surprised someone's taken him out, I'm surprised you hadn't run across him before though as he is, or was, a very bad boy."

"We live such sheltered lives out in the suburbs, but it now looks now as if I may get your job!"

"News travels fast around here but you are probably right, I'm getting a bit long in the tooth for getting my feet wet and looking at stiffs!"

"So what you reckon then?"

"Well I would say this is gang related and I wouldn't be at all surprised if you'll be seeing a few more floaters over the next few weeks."

After chatting about old times, Beaky leaves. Back at his car he finds he has a voice mail.

It's from Jenny.

STATION STREET

19.25

Station Street is unusual as there are no buildings. Station Street is a link road running behind factories and warehouses on one side with the rear of the City Fire Station on the other. The fire engines have another way into the yard, via a narrow side road. This is where Jenny and Beaky would meet after dark during their affair, which lasted for a couple of weeks. It wasn't that the DCC didn't love her husband, it was just that he prefers the lads to lassies, and after being discovered naked with his best friend on all fours, covered in boiled linseed oil on the potting shed floor, all three have all lived in perfect harmony ever since and have the best hydrangeas in the street. She has three strapping sons, all married to ladies.

Station Street has another advantage to would be lovers with nowhere to go, except the back seat of a Mondeo, because it has a very long deserted parking area. The reason for this is that the parking area was designed for trucks overnight, but someone in the planning department got their sums wrong and the street can only be accessed by light vehicles. One evening, a couple of years ago, Jenny borrowed a large camper van, but had to reverse back the length of Fire Street after attempting a twenty seven point turn.

When Beaky arrives, Jenny is already there sitting behind the wheel of a large black BMW. Our Detective Sergeant, parks his pink sports car and jumps out, locking it on the way round to the front passenger's door of the BMW.

"You took your time!"

"I came as soon as I could; I was doing your dirty work down at the slaughterhouse if you remember?"

"Do you know who he is?"

"Yes."

"How the hell are we going to live without you Plonkey?"

"You'll manage, that young bloke tonight thought he was indispensable, now he's just a lump of meat, anyway what have you got to tell me?"

"Well, I've got hold of her, she rang me back, thought that I was dying, got really upset.

She got even more upset when I told her about you!"

"What the hell did you tell her about me?"

"Shut up, I'm enjoying this! Well anyway, I told her that one of my boys, who has just retired, this detective, as a favour to a friend, is trying to trace you with news of your mother. At this she got a bit hysterical but I calmed her down and told her that her real mother did not want to meet her, just wanted to know that she was OK. I didn't say that you were Daddy X, but I think she may well put two and two together when she sees you!"

"So where is she then?"

"I told you to shut up! Anyway, I am coming to that, do you want the bad news first? Well of course you do, but it has a happy ending!"

Beaky wishes that a moment of bliss twenty five years ago had never happened.

"Now where was I? oh yes, it's not all happy families I'm afraid, although the adoptive parents did their best, she was the odd one out and became a very disruptive teenager getting into all kinds of trouble. At fifteen she ran away and had to be brought back, and then she disappeared for good. The next thing we hear is that she is in India and asking her adoptive parents to send her some money to get home. At this point the mother was very ill and the whole family decided to disown her. So there we are that's your lovely little daughter.

Oh yes, while out there she had a miscarriage and nearly died, but then things started to get better for her."

"How do you mean, this is the child from Hell, did she find spiritual enlightenment!"

"No, no, no, no, not at all, Mandy, that's her name by the way, was in a group of young drop outs and they all decided to come back overland on the Hippy Trail around thirty years after the real thing. Somewhere along the trail they got split up and she ended up in this mountain village, where the people were kind to her and she stayed there for about a year."

"And that changed her whole outlook on life and high on a mountain she found the meaning of life, a fairy godmother, a cave full of gold and an old rusty oil lamp?"

"If you are going to be silly Plonky then I won't tell you anymore. Actually, it was much better than that, because you see she learned something, she learned to do something that is unique to her, all through the help of this old lady in the village."

"You are making all this up!"

"Look, I've told you to keep quiet otherwise you will be on the wrong end of my truncheon! Keep losing my thread, ah yes, the old woman in the village"

"An old village woman showed her how to do something."

"Yes that's right, didn't I tell you to shut up?

Anyway this old lady was a potter and she showed Mandy how to make the most wonderful pots different and more colourful than anything seen in the West! So after a year, she made her way to Istanbul and eventually got home somehow.

She sold her story to a magazine and has started up her own pottery to make these things. I've told her that you will make a visit late tomorrow afternoon."

"I can see her in the morning, I could go now!"

"No, you can't, I think I deserve more than a peck on the cheek for what I've done for you and anyway you won't make it."

"Why's that?"

"Because she's at St. Bridgit's Well, a retreat high on the Moors."

"She's in a Convent, she's a nun?"

"No…..

She's in Cornwall!"

"That's not anywhere near Bournemouth!"

"Let's go in the back or would you rather recline your seat? I know you love the feel of cold leather on your cute little butt!"

"I'm not sure Jenny; I've got a long, hard journey tomorrow."

"But I can make it a lot quicker for you! Relax darling; you will see her tomorrow afternoon I promise, you just have to get your magic wand out and wave it about a bit."

"You mean she's coming up here?"

"No, you silly, silly boy, for a detective I'm rather surprised at you. Can't you see that I've just made the whole thing up because you are a very naughty little boy and you deserve to be punished by Auntie Jennifer!

If I remember, you rather like being punished!

She's an accountant by the way, goes by the name of Sarah.

She lives a boring accountant's life in Northampton."

BOSCOMBE

Friday 8th May 09.45

Angela is upset, not only is the old lady talking constantly about babies, but Beaky failed to call last night. OK, they are not an item, but for the first time in her life she thinks she may be in love? Not in a soppy, Hollywood, let's wear matching sweaters and call each other Mummy and Daddy, sort of way, but a 'let's see what happens now' sort of way. Angela needs to get out of the stifling apartment block full of old people shuffling around and fighting over the use of the tumble dryer.

Angela wants to find some criminals and arrest them.

With this in mind, she takes a Yellow Bus to Boscombe, she's the only one who has to pay. The bus is loaded with old people. The old lady sitting next to her recommends a couple of charity shops that are good for flat shoes and sensible underwear. OMG, thinks Angela, Beaky wants me to live in this cemetery!

But Boscombe comes as a surprise. Long gone are the large department stores and many of the elegant houses are now flats. The primrose and maroon trolleys no longer swish down Main Street, which has been shut to traffic and has a bright open market twice every week. Unfortunately, this piece of Council forward thinking is now home to buskers and beggars. The police are friendly; in fact everyone is friendly because there's a sort of buzz about the place. Second hand shops rub shoulders with discount stores, banks and cafes. It's noisy, fun and surprisingly litter free, at least on the main drag. Angela is coming alive, breathing in the salt laden air. She makes her way down Sea Road to the pier. On the pier, she finds a seat in the central shelter and calls Beaky. His 'phone is off, but after a short while, he calls back.

"Sorry Angie Poos, I was driving on the Motorway, pulled in now for a coffee."

"Are you coming back today, what's the news?"

"Look, I don't want to get your hopes up, I've got a lead and I'm on my way to Northampton, I may be late back, can I stay with you at Auntie's?"

"No problem, don't tell me any more, I don't want to get my hopes up and one other thing, thank you, I love you, but you've always known that haven't you?"

Angela walks off the pier and takes the Undercliff Drive towards Bournemouth. On the way back to the apartment, she buys the local paper. On one of the inside pages, a small headline jumps out at her…..

DORSET MAN FOUND DEAD IN CAR AT ROUND BAY

CENTRAL BOURNEMOUTH

12.10

Angela helps Auntie out of the car and walks her quickly around the corner and up to the main door of the Police Station.

"Right, go on in!"

"But I don't want to!"

"Go on and please try to look like a little old lady."

"But I am a little old lady!"

"Yes I know you are but please try a little harder, I told you to stoop, now take the stick and go inside!"

"I don't want the stick, I don't use a stick!"

"Well you do now, and practice the voice, a bit like Margaret Rutherford now can you remember what to say? Let's go through it again."

"I ask the officer about my late cousin Joe, who's been found dead, I read about it in the paper, I know he had a bad heart, is that what's killed him?"

"Yes, that will do, now off you go, and stoop, oh for God's sake stoop!"

Angela watches as Auntie limps up to the desk and speaks to a young PC. Then, an even younger WPC comes out and has a few words with her. Auntie rushes back to the door in triumph, quite forgetting that she is an old lady. After dragging her back and stuffing Auntie into the low slung car, Angela wants to know what they told her.

"Well they are not allowed to say until they've had a ferret around inside him, if you get my drift? If you want my opinion, it was caused by your boyfriend putting the frighteners on him!"

"You read too many crime novels and he's NOT my boyfriend!"

"Then why have you been searching out Estate Agents down here?"

"I've just been looking in the windows."

DANIEL, COOMBES & SCRANT

13.45

One advantage the inhabitants of Northampton have over the rest of us is that they can find their way around their town centre. After a struggle and a long walk, Beaky eventually washes up at the door of Daniel, Coombes & Scrant (Accountants). He is immediately shown into the cosy, rather old fashioned office of Ms Sarah Finch, who is basically a young Beaky in a skirt doing a very good impression of Llandudno.

Sarah is, like her old man, immaculately dressed. She wears a power suit, perfectly cut in medium grey with a touch of herring bone. The skirt is very short complemented by black tights and white killer heels. The part of this ensemble that takes Beaky's eye however, is the white blouse, because inside the open collar is a cravat! Not like his silver and pink spotted one, more a lady type British Airways inspired, loosely tied scarf with wavy stripes. Beaky is impressed, definitely a chip off the old block! Sarah walks up to him, grips his right hand firmly and tries to rip his shoulder out from its socket.

"Good afternoon James, Auntie has told me all about you. Please sit down and tell me about my God awful mother? The evil one who left me in the hospital."

Beaky clears his throat and says in a voice as smooth as velvet over satin.

"Yes, I know your mother, she's a friend, and the woman has problems. She lost her sister when a little girl, and then soon after, her own mother died in an institution. Her father, who was a religious nutcase, disowned her even though she had risen to the rank of Police Sergeant at the time. She had no one to turn to, the baby's father had gone off and she didn't love him, so the force closed ranks, and found you a loving couple who desperately wanted a baby and by the look of it, you've turned out alright!"

"By God, you know how to charm the ladies, I was warned about! You are something else. Take my advice though, ditch the cravat; you look like a Pox Doctor's Tart's Maid at a Torquay Tea Dance!

I'm sorry, and I don't mean to be bitter, it's not your fault, you are just the messenger."

She examines him closely,

"Or maybe it is your fault? Look I've got clients to see and work to do, I'll meet you around six at The Old Tram in Fisher Street, change into something a bit more casual or you may get picked up and have a life changing experience!

You can buy me dinner Daddy, as you've left it a bit late to take me to the Zoo."

THE OLD TRAMCAR WINE BAR

18.30

Sarah is late and this is causing problems for Beaky's manhood.

The Old Tramcar is not the place to hang around on your own for too long, unless you are looking for something. Beaky has already been eyed up by the regulars and is trying to concentrate on the evening paper. He also needs to get going as he wants to be back in Bournemouth tonight. An elderly man, wearing a leather hat and a T shirt emblazoned with, 'Everybody loves a Cowgirl' slides over to his table and asks in a Texan drawl,

"Waiting for someone in par dic u lar Pardner?"

Beaky, now in self destruct mode, breathes,

"Doris Day, coming in on the Deadwood Stage tonight."

Around seven, after four Diet Cokes with ice, Sarah appears and sits down opposite.

"You are late!"

"You are twenty five bloody years too late!"

They order the pasta with cheese topping, Sarah drinks too much house wine.

Beaky hopes his little girl is not driving.

Beaky explains a bit more about the past and asks if he can take her picture?

Sarah declines but promises to send one on to him.

Sarah does not reveal much about herself; apart from that her adoptive parents were kind. She went to college and now she's a fully fledged accountant and financial adviser, between lovers and more interested in her career than commitment at present. Her Mum and Dad have retired to the Isle of Wight and she sees them two or three times a year.

When Beaky tells her that her real mum does not want to make contact, Sarah seems pleased.

For two people who have never met before, the evening is going well. Beaky thinks she is sweet and Sarah thinks her new Dad is funny.

Half way through the evening, Beaky's 'phone rings; it's Angela.

"Where are you, and what's all that noise?"

"I'm tied up in a rather gay bar in Northampton but should be back tonight.

" I'm not sure what time I will arrive."

"Well be quiet and don't wake up the old people, ring me from the Spur Road and I'll come down and let you in. Have you found her?"

"Yes and she's all right, works as an accountant, she's going to send a nice picture, that's all you want isn't it?"

There's a long pause and then Angela says quietly,

"Yes, yes that's all I want, thanks but come on back, something's happened and you are too old to hang around in bars, once you had found her you should have started back."

"What's happened?"

"I think we can forget about this business with my sister, your prime witness is dead, they found him at Round Bay sitting in his car, so we will never know what he had to say."

"You're wrong there Poo Poos, he sent me a note, got it this morning. I'll tell you about it when I get back and I'm quite safe I'm in a singles bar full of elderly lesbians and transvestites!"

At this point the 'Cowgirl' arrives, grabs Beaky's 'phone and says in a high camp voice,

"He's quite safe love, he's with Doris Day!"

FOX VALE

Saturday 9th May 11.30

Beaky gets back around two in the morning and sleeps in until eleven. He is in a yellow dressing gown, supplied by Auntie. He hands Angela the note.

"So you want to retrieve this box with the statement inside it, wouldn't that be dangerous?"

"Not at all, there's nothing suspicious about the death and no one is going to connect us with a disappearance that took place 43 years ago!"

"Are we going after dark?"

"No, in broad daylight, but we'll go on Sunday; I don't want to run into that overzealous parking snoop, and just in case, we'll take my car."

"A pink MX5 with pop up headlights, do you think that's wise Barbie?"

"Perhaps we should hire a white Corsa or Polo? Something bland, something that won't stand out, we'll take one of those supermarket bags for life to put the cashbox in."

"Why do you want the cashbox?"

"Dunno, just have a feeling about it, after all, why not just put the envelope in the space under the floor?

"Anyway, what were you doing in a gay bar, having a life changing Llandudno moment?"

"I was with our daughter if you must know. It was just a nice place to go."

"For a new Dad to take his daughter to? I just don't believe you sometimes!"

"Why not? She's a lovely girl, looks just like me! Let's just say we got on fine, I won't say any more because I know that you are not interested, and you know Poo Poos, quite a lot of my fellow officers think that you might be a bit on the lesbian side as you don't normally seem to like us men very much."

 "Be careful what you say in front of Auntie!"

Auntie looks up from her knitting.......

 "Oh don't mind me dear, I know all about that sort of thing, in fact I was a lesbian for a short time."

"Does your boyfriend know about this?"

"Of course my dear!

We don't keep secrets at our age, Bill tells me that he once had a very interesting experience in Portsmouth."

"So when were you a lesbian?"

"It was when I was at boarding school, all very innocent, her name was Anne and we used to lie naked in the apple store after Sunday prayers.

We would hold hands and recite 'Hiawatha'."

WOOLHAM

Sunday 10ᵗʰ May 10.05

Angela drives the new Corsa down the twisting country lanes on this beautiful late spring morning. The hot sun makes dappled patterns on the road through the waving branches of trees in full leaf, as they pass pretty cottage gardens and neat farms. For once in her life she feels truly happy, she knows her daughter is out there, a real person, not a shadow, and she hopes the day may bring an answer to the fate of her sister.

Beaky is very quiet, deep in thought.

Angela breaks the silence.

"Do you now think he killed her?"

"Not sure, I was convinced she ran away, it's just this cashbox, was it from the post office? Did he steal from his parents? Why has he felt so guilty all of these years? I'm sure that there was something going on between those two, maybe he got cold feet?"

"Maybe they fell out and he killed her, trying to shut her up? Maybe he dragged her down the beach, hid the body and went back later to bury it?"

"Maybe, but that's too simple for me, I just have this feeling that there is a lot more to it, we are clutching at straws."

At Woolham, the cobbled square is empty and most of the shops are shut. They leave the car in a side street and walk round to Joe's Emporium, gaining access to the rear via a narrow dank alleyway. The key turns effortlessly in the lock and the door is pushed open. Inside, the windowless room is dark and uncomfortable. Beaky searches for the light switch.

The table is larger than he remembers and he needs Angela's help to move it. He kneels down, and with the help of a screwdriver, eases up the two floorboards. Reaching down he feels around for the box, it is smaller than he imagined and the hasp has been cut through. Beaky lifts the box out onto the floor and retrieves the large envelope, which he passes to Angela. He then carefully replaces the floorboards. They lift the heavy table back to it's original position and quietly leave the premises, Angela holding on to the envelope, Beaky with the steel box hidden in the supermarket bag.

They drive to a quiet spot.

Angela opens the envelope.

"Read it," says Beaky.

Dear Sergeant Parrot

I will leave you to decide what to do, you may wish to destroy this statement, then again, you may wish to take things further as I believe the Police rarely close a case. What I am about to tell you is true and I remember every detail as though it was yesterday. I first met Jasmine Sadler when the family called in at the post office on their way to Round Bay on the first day of their holiday. I was immediately attracted to her, as she was very pretty. While her parents and the little girl were deciding what supplies they needed, we stepped outside and we had a conversation, which led to a rendezvous on the beach that evening. Her father was a strange man and only let her out for short periods even though she told me that she would be eighteen on the following Saturday.

We met each evening for an hour and, being young, I became besotted by her and by Wednesday she had told me, in secret, that on Saturday (her birthday) she would be free and she was off! Over the next two evenings, she filled me in on her plan and asked me to go with her, not on Saturday, but later when she was settled. She was a bit vague as to where she was going, but said she was starting a new job in London. My part in all this was to lay a false trail when her father realised she had gone. She asked me to hang around the guest house on Saturday morning and I noticed that the mother and the sister being taken out in an old car. Then shouting coming from the house and Jasmine came out crying and took me off down to the beach.

She told me the old man was going out for the afternoon, he wouldn't say where, and as soon as he went, she was going back to her bedroom to get something. After he left, she came back with the tin cash box. Apparently, he ran his own business and was very tight with money. Although religious, he did not like paying tax, so all of his cash went with him wherever he happened to be. This particular afternoon he thought it was locked up in his car, but unbeknown to him she had a spare key made and had taken it out when he wasn't looking. The box was (and still is) locked with a large padlock. Jasmine asked me to saw through the hasp and gave me a brand new 12" hacksaw with two new heavy duty blades. She told me to cut through the steel, which was quite hard to do, stuff all the money inside into a bag and meet her at the bus stop on

Poacher's Corner, a remote spot around five miles away. I was to get rid of the box and the saw.

Well I did this, temporarily hiding the box and saw behind the chicken house. Inside the box I found around £4000, a fortune then. I met her at the bus stop with the money and she gave me £200 back. We kissed and she promised to let me know when I could join her. She told me not to wait for the bus, so I will never know if she got on it. I waited for her to contact me, but after a month, I knew she had used me. I had committed a terrible crime by taking the money. My last job was to ride my bike back to the beach and stay there for a couple of hours.

If asked, I was to say that I saw a young lady wading out into the sea.

And that's what I eventually told the Police.

ROUND BAY

14.00

Angela drives in silence; her right hand gripping the statement, Beaky talks to himself most of the way. He was getting there but he should have realised that Jasmine Sadler had a cruel streak like her father. He thinks she is still around somewhere and although Joe did not see her board the bus, he's pretty certain she got away. The old man was probably relieved although losing the money would have hurt deeply. He couldn't report it as people would have become suspicious, he probably had more stashed away, although Angela never saw any of it. At the car park by the Round Bay Hotel, Angela asks him to come down to the beach with her. She reaches down, hands Beaky her handbag and asks him to carry it.

"I'm not happy about doing that!"

"You didn't seem to mind in Llandudno so I'm told!"

"I wish I could remember Llandudno!"

At the water's edge, Angela removes her shoes and wades into the water.

"Come on in the tides running out we can go a long way!"

"Don't be silly Poo Poos!"

"It's OK I'm not going to do anything silly, quite the reverse in fact, something I should have done a long time ago, bury the dead!"

Angela is racing out into the sea with a reluctant Beaky stumbling behind, his tender feet treading on the sharp stones. When the cold water reaches over her knees, Angela stops and waits for Beaky, who being that much shorter, is in some distress. They gaze out towards the ocean; Angela rips up the statement and offers it to the wind. The pieces fly off towards the sun, they rise up into the sky and then they are gone, as if they had never existed. Angela asks for her handbag, opens it and takes out the picture of her and her sister. She passes it to Beaky.

"Let it go, I know now that she's never coming back, let it go."

Beaky drops it onto the water, where it floats for a second or two before a wave takes it away.

At 97A Brandon Street, a large envelope drops onto the door mat.

Inside is a photograph of a young lady. There is also a letter inside a small pink envelope on the front of which are written two words…

"Dear Mum."

Too far out to see me waving,

Too far out to catch your eye,

Too far out for you to find me,

Too far out to hear me cry.

Too far out for you to touch me,

Too far out to hold my hand,

Too far out for you to find me,

Too far out beyond the sand.

Illustration: Amber Cooke

One Month Later ...

Angela and Beaky have now been released from the Police Force and are living in Angela's apartment, which is on the market for £450000. Being a single girl, a workaholic and having no distractions away from the coalface, she has paid off the mortgage. Beaky's small flat sold within three days at a good profit, so with their pensions they are pretty well set up to move to the seaside and mature slowly like old wine in a nice little bungalow.

Oh, if only life were that simple!

The idea is that Beaky can then set up his detective agency and Angela will be his 'Man Friday'. Beaky is hopeless with money and any sort of organised life, so Angela will run the business on a day to day basis and help out on cases, a sort of Dr Watson to his Mr Holmes. Angela, of course, will never be able to take second place to a man and the relationship will always be a difficult one, but for the first time in her life she has started to mellow a little. This has been caused by her daughter writing to her, and although it will be a long time before they meet, if ever, the ice is starting to melt between them. Sarah has persuaded her mother to go onto Social Media, so Angela now has more than one photograph of her, and Auntie has a big one in a silver frame over the fireplace, or where one would be if there was a fireplace in her living room.

Beaky has been helping his old mates down at the nick with an interesting case of false identity when, out of the blue, Jenny Mannings (now Acting Chief Constable) leaves a message for him to meet her in Station Street.

STATION STREET

Monday 15th June 11.45

Once again, the black BMW is parked up snugly to the kerb in the long lay-by. Beaky doesn't want anyone to see his pink sports car in broad daylight, so takes a cab to the Fire Station. Jenny can't resist giving him a kiss, despite the fact that it would make the front page of every Sunday scandal sheet. Jenny drives out of the City and they pull off the road into a small wood, Beaky strongly suspects that she's been here before.

Beaky, now almost a married man, prepares to sacrifice himself for England and the New City Division, but gets a shock when the Chief asks him to keep his pants on. What she has to say hits him like a sledgehammer; he has made a mistake, a big one!

"You have been very naughty once again Plonkey, sticking your little beak into other people's business. So far there are now three people, possibly four, who have died since your little episode with Madam up at the stately home, how many more are going to end up on a slab?"

"I don't know what you are talking about?"

"Oh yes you do, don't play innocent with me, I had a call from my old mate Brian last night, he's now in charge down south. A man has died in his car, had a massive heart attack but they can't find out what brought this on, his GP had given him another ten years if he moved out to the sun and took it easy."

"What the hell has this got to do with me? People die all the time!"

"It's because you paid him a visit a few days before!"

"You can't prove that."

"Oh yes we can because you were driving Angie's car and and the overzealous car parking Gestapo jotted down the number and took a photo of it, after taking you to this guy's shop. Code CZ RED, remember? When he heard that the shopkeeper had died, ever helpful as a paid up member of the your so called 'Enforcing Establishment' he 'phoned the police!"

Beaky's response to all this is not what Jenny expects.

"That's it! That's it, I couldn't see the wood for the trees, a false trail it was much too neat! Oh thanks Jenny, you've solved the crime, why was I so stupid? No need to tell Poo Poos, she's happy now, but I need to clear this up! I think I know where Jasmine might be!"

"Now take you trousers and pants off and put on this policeman's helmet."

14.30

Beaky, still wearing his striped sports jacket has been tied to a tree, sans trousers and underpants, by Jenny who has abandoned him to his fate. After around an hour of wriggling, he manages to break free and calls the Plod, asking if someone can bring him a pair of trousers and underpants.

 When asked why? He replies,

"An unexpected bowel movement in the forest."

Before she left, Jenny asked him to sort this out, as she's asked Brian not to take the matter further.

 Beaky is elated; he can see where he went wrong.

The joy of the chase is so much more important to a detective than an exposed bottom.

The boys and girls in blue arrive in three police cars, lights blazing fiercely and sirens wailing. They fix him up with an old pair of jeans, two sizes too small, left by a drunk. Just for fun, instead of underpants, Hilda has donated a lacy pair of large knickers. Beaky, with due ceremony, ties the knickers to a tree branch, in case some other poor soul may have need of them. They take him home, but he insists on walking (with great difficulty) the last two blocks.

Beaky is in luck. When he gets back to Angela's apartment, she's out. He quickly swaps trousers and rushes downstairs to put the jeans in the communal bin.

When Angela gets back, he suggests that he goes down to Bournemouth at the weekend to look at property.

"Anything in mind?" asks a quite buoyant Angela.

Beaky is prepared and shows her the first one that's come up on his lap top.

"Looks divine darling, you go and visit Auntie at the same time," she says and then explains why she can't go. Things are starting to go right for Beaky today, after a rough start.

"The girls are giving me a farewell bash at Barringtons in Fishgate. It will be a bitchy affair as they all hate me, but I'd thought I'd go, apparently there will be strippers and an old bloke called Cyril who jumps out of a cake, wearing nothing but a pink marigold on his tiny willy! You should see the invite from your girlfriend; it came in on my phone this afternoon. There's a bloke tied up to a tree completely naked from the waist down. He's wearing a striped jacket just like yours Mr Plonkey!

FAIRFIELD VILLAGE

Saturday 20th June 09.00

Beaky has hired a white Transit van for the day, he has asked
for the oldest one available. He has parked it under a tree in a
passing place back down the narrow lane. Beaky watches from
behind a line of conifers, planted as a windbreak in this bleak
spot, to see if Hamlin is in. Beaky has casually asked Angela,
what car Hamlin drives and notices that the ugly green Micra is
sitting patiently in one of the much fought over car park spaces.
At around 10.15, Hamlin appears from number five and walks
to his car. The nearest large store is at least ten miles of bad
road away. Beaky hopes the old man is going shopping and
there will be enough time to get in and out of his tiny home
before he returns.

As soon as he sees the Micra vanish over the hill, Beaky
returns to the van and potters down to the village. He parks just
inside the complex. Dressed in a smart, clean pair of grey
overalls, looking nothing like a tradesman and carrying a
canvas tool bag last seen in a silent movie; he makes his way
along the path that serves the rear gardens of the tiny
bungalows. He walks up to the kitchen door of number five and
from a large bunch of keys, selects one which may free the
lock. Before actually inserting said key however, he notices a
large empty plant pot by the door. He puts his hand deep into
the pot and brings out a key tied to a length of dirty string. He
lets himself in and quietly goes through the place looking in all
the drawers and cupboards. Luckily, Hamlin has left the
curtains shut.

Beaky places the metal cash box gently onto the dining table.

On the way back to the van he meets the warden, a formidable looking woman with an army haircut, combat boots, sagging breasts and military moustache.

"Are you authorised?" she barks.

"Of course me dear," Beaky replies in a Dorset accent straight out of Central Casting,

"You can tell Master Mills that I've found what I was looking for, it's all done now."

With that, Beaky reverses out onto the narrow road, swings the Transit around and drives sedately up the hill.

On the way out he passes a green Micra plodding the opposite way.

BARRINGTONS

22.00

Barringtons was built in the late 70s as a ten pin bowling centre. Unfortunately by this time the American craze was cooling down, and as it was in the city centre, with city centre prices, it was far too expensive for English kids. Since then it has become the place to be seen and because of its huge pillar free warehouse like interior, it has turned into a very popular venue for hen and stag parties.

Angela is falling out of a skimpy little black number with lots of bling and for her age looks pretty good compared with some of her contemporary crime fighting sisters. She has decided to keep off the booze and let the others make fools of themselves. Strong drink loosens up the tongue and she waits to hear some 'home truths' emerge about her. To Angela's surprise this does not happen, although after half a dozen vodkas Jenny tells everybody whose bum was on the invite.

The stripping team, known as the 'Gay Boy Minstrels', are a bit of a disappointment as their balloons prove rather difficult to burst. As luck would have it, PC Hilda Fosset has a large, industrial cigarette lighter in her handbag and this is causing a few Brazilian screams among the younger boys. This leads to an unwanted premature discharge of a large fire extinguisher. At this point, the Manager threatens to throw them all out, but as he has 'form' he changes his mind after Jenny takes him firmly in hand in the vestibule.

Angela shares a taxi home with the Acting Chief Constable and asks if she had intercourse with Beaky in the wood today?

Jenny replies that it was a bit too public, and he settled for a slap.

As Jenny attempts to leave the confines of the cab, she surprises Angela by saying,

"Don't worry about our Mr Plonkey my love, he's yours, he always has been, he'd lay down his life for you, you know that. Yes, he's fully serviced most of us ladies in the Division over the years, and we all love and appreciate him, but he was always yours and always will be. You see he loves women, understands us, in some ways he's a bit of an old woman himself! Have you ever noticed how good a driver he is? He knows just what to do, whatever the situation and he's the same in bed. So look after him, otherwise you will upset the sisterhood and your dream bungalow in Bournemouth will need wheelchair access!"

At this point, the Chief Constable collapses in the road.

APARTMENT 22

GLENVILLE TOWERS

Sunday 21st June 07.14

Angela wakes refreshed. Although plied with numerous drinks last night, she managed to leave half of them on various tables around the room, and took the rest on her many trips to the toilet. She also bribed the barmaid to keep a large glass of water out of sight for her to drink when no one was looking. After midnight it didn't matter anyway, as most of the middle aged women were too far gone to notice.

Angela finally got to bed around three and has had a short, but deep sleep. The dream has returned, but this time it's kind to her, in soft focus. Her father has gone and Jazz is a distant figure on land rising beyond the sea. Then suddenly she is there, inside the room, standing by the door. Angela is not frightened any more; she knows this is just a dream.

Jazz starts to fade.

And she knows that it will be the last time she will ever see her.

FAIRFIELD VILLAGE

11.00

Beaky gently taps on the door of number five.

Hamlin opens the door and blinks into the strong sunlight.

"Come in, I was expecting you."

He makes tea and they sit opposite each other, Beaky goes to show some ID but Hamlin tells him to put it away.

"You are a policeman?"

"Retired."

"How did you know?"

"Angela, the ex Chief Inspector, is a friend of mine, and when she told me that cock and bull story you furnished upon her, I knew no policeman of your experience, whatever his or her rank would try and palm that off as the truth, unless it was to a vulnerable person who was clutching at straws and was willing to believe anything. I knew it was a cover up, but after 43 years the trail had gone cold. Then Joe made his statement and left me the cash box to throw me off the scent and that was just too neat. What really puzzled me was why Joe should get into such a state to bring on the heart attack that killed him; after all in his statement all he had done was to steal a small sum of money. It just didn't add up. Then I got to thinking that if he had killed her, he could not have disposed of the body by himself, there must have been someone else, someone who nobody would have ever expected, and someone who was there to protect the community and uphold the law. I've had a look at the old police house, I found out it's been empty since you left and it's up for sale again. It's still a little remote from the village, with an enclosed rear garden, the perfect spot to hide a body!"

"How did you know for sure that I was involved?"

"Well I was not sure but I heard last week that a nasty snooping little Jobsworth in Woolham had taken a picture of the car I was driving and that got me thinking about Jasmine. In the photograph that Angela had showed me she was wearing a necklace and I recognised it immediately as it was an unusual and quite rare Welsh design in the form of a Celtic cross, not the sort of thing a Bible thumping, Old Testament hellfire, puritanical and miserly father would give to his daughter. When I worked in North Wales years ago I remember seeing one of these necklaces for sale, it was quite expensive. Finding an identical one here yesterday and a lock of hair that could help to identify any remains I admit was a bonus. I've checked up and found that your wife had left some time before so you were living there alone. It all seemed to fit into place.

I believe that you had met Jasmine the year before and on the day of her death she had spent the afternoon at the police house. The one thing I can't figure is what this cash box has to do with any of this and how Joe got involved? Did he unwittingly walk in, perhaps with a delivery from the shop?"

"I'm afraid it is much, much simpler than that, most things in life are, but I didn't kill her, how could I? I loved her, I still do. Jasmine arrived on my doorstep with a suitcase; she wanted us to run away together. I asked her to wait until I could get a transfer to another place far away. There was no rush as we had the rest of our lives to be together. At this point, she became hysterical and ran out of the house and along the narrow lane towards the village. It was Joe who killed her. He came out of nowhere driving the shop delivery van at breakneck speed; he had only passed his test the week before. The funny thing is that there were no marks on her, not even a trace of blood, but I knew she was dead. I did what I could but there was no pulse, she had gone. I told Joe to take the van back before his nerve went then run back to the house. While he was gone, I dragged the body round the back and started to dig a grave. Later that evening we buried her deep in the garden, along with the suitcase, and threw a lot of rubble, that was lying about, on top of her. I told Joe to make a statement and say he saw a girl walking in the sea."

"And the metal box? Joe said it was her father's, where he kept his money."

"The box was mine, standard issue to Village Bobbies at the time; it was where I kept her letters. After her death I couldn't bear to keep it in the Police House, so I asked Joe to look after it. As the years went by I realised that I would never be able to read them again and I asked Joe, just before I moved here, to dispose of the box. He obviously got curious, cut the box open and destroyed the letters."

Beaky takes the bracelet and lock of hair out of his pocket, places them into the box and closes the lid.

"What are you going to do now?"

"Nothing, Joe is dead, and Angela has moved on, the case is closed."

After a long pause, Beaky asks,

"What will you do?"

Hamlin, looks out to sea and replies,

"I'm an old man, my time is short. I still visit the garden every week, as I have done for the past 43 years, the most beautiful flowers grow up there. I've instructed my solicitor to have my ashes scattered over the garden, we will be together once more."

"And if the new people move in before this happens?"

"One day I'll go down to the beach.

And walk in the sea."

All books by Barrie Haynes
are available from
AMAZON BOOKSTORE UK
or contact the author
www.barriehaynes.wordpress.com

Printed in Great Britain
by Amazon

86500076R10063